Lock Down Publications and Ca$h
Presents

I0637456

THE
Dirty Side Of
MONEY 2
Root Of All Evil

Written By
PRINCE
The Obsessive Gritty and Raw Urban/Street Crime Author

First Edition 2025

Printed in the United States of America

This is a work of fiction. Names, characters, places, and incidents either
are products of the author's imagination or are used fictitiously. Any
similarity to actual events or locales or persons, living or dead, is
entirely coincidental.

Lock Down Publications
P.O. Box 944
Stockbridge, GA 30281
www.lockdownpublications.com

Like our page on Facebook: Lock Down Publications
www.facebook.com/lockdownpublications.ldp

Stay Connected with Us!

Text **LOCKDOWN** to 22828 to stay up-to-date with new releases, sneak peaks, contests and more…

Like our page on Facebook:
Lock Down Publications

Join Lock Down Publications/The New Era Reading Group

Visit our website:
www.lockdownpublications.com

Follow us on Instagram:
Lock Down Publications

Email Us: We want to hear from you!

AUTHOR'S NOTE

To my readers, both day-ones and those just now tapping in. I want to thank you for choosing to enter the worlds I create. Worlds that are dark, gritty, raw, and unflinching in their realism. I don't sugarcoat not a goddamn thing! I don't romanticize. I write what's real. I tell the kind of stories that don't always get told, especially not from the perspective of a Black man as myself that is navigating the streets, the game, trauma, power, betrayal, and the war for legacy.

What I do ain't just fiction. This shit is survival!

Truth is, being a Black male author in the lit game feels a lot like fighting in the Hunger Games. It's a ruthless battlefield. A war zone, even. The urban fiction industry is dominated by women—female authors, female readers, and female-centered narratives. And while there's respect for that, it leaves cats like myself out in the cold. There ain't many lanes for us. No real support systems. No safety nets. No open arms. Just a sharp pen, raw vision, and a will to out-write and outlast, and to be more prepared.

I'm not here to compete with my lit brothers. (or my lit sisters for that matter) I'm here to build something bigger than me. But the way this industry is set up, they pit us against each other. Like only one of us can make it at a time. Like there's only room for one voice, one pen, one brand. That's a lie. And I'm here to challenge it.

So when you support my books, you're doing more than reading stories. You're breaking a cycle. You're making space for a voice that ain't supposed to exist in this format. Especially not so from the current predicament that I find myself. You're saying: his stories matters, too.

4

This journey ain't easy. But it's necessary. And as long as I got breath and fire in me, I'll keep pushing this pen, writing for the voiceless, the forgotten, the misunderstood, and the feared. And my pen is fire! It's lethal!

Thank you for riding with me.

—Prince (smile)

P.S. To **REALLY** support what I do, buy a book (or books) and buymeacoffee.com/PrinceThaAuthor (smile). I run on caffeine, obsession, anger, pain, emotions, and the will to win at all cost. Once again, thank you for everything!

"For the love of money is the root of all evil!"
(Holy Bible— I Timothy Ch.6: V. 10)

Prologue

Verena, her mother, and Eric settled in well in the 7-bedroom, 4 bath, 2,700 square foot mini-mansion they'd bought in Princeton, New Jersey. Business was going good for the two, as Eric had gotten into the real estate market and began flipping houses. He had also put his money into buying into a couple of restaurant franchises—White Castle—as this was a popular food chain in the state. For the few months he and Verena had been up north, Eric had really flourished to becoming a shrewd businessman and was making progress in a multitude of ways. He'd taken the money from the tax schemes he and Montell and the crew had put together, along with all the money Verena cuffed on Montell, and truly made good use of it.

He expressed his desires to Verena, "I got plans and have had visions, to be the owner of a company, that would make me a very rich man someday. And I'm gonna make good use of you, Verena, and all the credentials you carry along with having degrees and being the former warden over a prison."

"I'm all for it, sweetheart. And I'm down with you."

However, times changed. He had her co-sign on a lot. Eric played it smart on Verena as well, by having separate bank accounts from hers and stashing cash in locales she had no knowledge of. He figured if she would cross Montell to be with him in the way she had, who's to say she wouldn't do him the same way with some other guy? So, Eric felt the need to play it safe.

Not only that, Verena had become a real bitch towards Eric now, throughout her pregnancy. She also began to eat more than she should, and picked up a few pounds that would be hard to shred, once she dropped her load. She had become somewhat unattractive in Eric's eyes, and annoying in a major way, by questioning him often about his whereabouts and the things he was up to. By all means, she had begun to run him away.

But he played things cool for the most part, as he had an end game in the making. And to think he had once strongly considered making Verena his wife. But her pressure campaign on him to do so, forced him to continue on putting things off. Besides, he had a couple other females on the side he dealt with. Nonetheless, he still had a deep love for Verena.

"Eric, baby," She called out to him one night as they began to prepare for bed. "I think it's about time we began to come up with some potential names for our twins," she said to him. She was seven months pregnant with a boy and a girl. It showed like no other.

"Rena, we still got plenty of time left to do all this. Ain't no need to rush it," Eric replied.

"I know baby. I know. But you know how I am. I just like to have things handled way ahead of time," she mentioned.

"Verena, look. You not the warden over the prison any longer, babe. You can relax a little. It's going to be okay," he responded. "I got you baby."

"I'm just excited for us. That's all."

"Yeah, me too. But I just need for you to relax and be easy," Eric said.

"I'm trying to, but I can't. My hormones and my thoughts of you wont allow me to," she said, and gently stroked on his arm as he had on a wife-beater. She then caressed on his thigh, stopping at his manhood, massaging it to life, hoping he would finally fuck her, as it had been over thirty days since he last gave the dick to Verena.

Her cellphone rang as it sat on the nightstand next to the bed charging. It was Tiffany. The two had finally reconnected not long before the day. That was Eric's cue to get up and head to his man-cave he'd made for himself in the basement. He wanted to watch some music videos, shoot a few rounds of pool to himself, and sip on good champagne to relax his mind. Eric suffered from a terrible case of insomnia and from the effects of Adderall use. He had experienced many sleepless nights and moments out of bed. And Verena hated it with a passion.

Her mother stayed there in the house with them too and would often hear them argue or fucking. Nonetheless, Mrs. Deanne, was okay with everything her daughter and her boyfriend had going on, being that she knew Verena had been deprived of having a personal life and a boyfriend growing up. She had no sibling sister to look up to and learn from about dating and having a boyfriend. And Momma Dee remembered Eric from day one.

Verena didn't begin having sex until she neared graduating high school. Then again when she got to college. But that didn't last too long, because she was too focused on having a career and trying to live up to the expectations her parents had placed upon her. So, guys and getting dick was out of the question.

***

For a long time, Verena's mother thought maybe she was into females and not males, because Verena was not in tune heavily with her feminine side in the way her mother and other women folk of her family was. Also, Verena never talked to her mother about guys, never asked for tips on how to keep a man sexually satisfied, or how to keep a man happy period. Let alone bring one by the house for mother's approval. Not until that first time with Eric.

The only person Mrs. Deanne had remotely saw Verena very close to or possibly stimulated by sexually, was the friend, Tiffany, as they had taken baths together, slept together on sleep overs, and had saw, along with touched on, each other's naked bodies one too many times to count.

Verena's mother noticed a dramatic change in her at the point of not being able to have Tiffany as close to her or staying over as she always had, once they'd reached adulthood. And Mrs. Deanne, also observed a jealous type of behavior out of Verena, when Tiffany had gotten married and had to provide her husband with all the "intimate" time she once gave to Verena. It appeared as if Verena had caught feelings and was in love with Tiffany, a love she coveted wanted back, but couldn't have.

But as time passed, Mrs. Deanne paid Verena no more mind and felt before long, she would finally reveal what she had an appetite for males or females to do the nasty with. Then, Eric popped upon the scene, and Verena ended up pregnant with twins. This concluded any speculations Mrs. Deanne may have held.

"What's up Tiffany. How you been, girl?" Verena answered her phone.

"I'm good girl. How you been?" the friend replied.

"Everything okay for the time being. I just don't know what to make of Eric, girl. He's so hard to figure out and to pinpoint, Tiffany. I just don't know," She had mentioned.

"Well, what is he doing that causes you to feel the way you do?"

"He don't pay me any attention anymore. He don't compliment me like he used to. And he don't even fuck me on the regular no more. We ain't had sex in over thirty days girl. He tells me, I'm too controlling, and I demand too much! *Dafuq!*"

"Have you took heed of all he has said? Did you take time out to at least think about that for a moment?"

"Tiffany! What are you trying to tell me, sista girl? Huh."

"What I'm trying to tell you is that, maybe your mood swings associated with your pregnancy, has been causing you to be someone that you truly not. And by him not giving you the sex you've grown to love so much, that's just his way of temporarily punishing you until you earn it back, or until you simply take it back as his woman," Tiffany informed.

"Yeah, you probably got a point there, Tiffany. Maybe I have been a bit overwhelming. Maybe I have been a *bitch* towards him I don't need to be or mean to be. It's just that, I'm not good at this relationship thing, girl. And I'm forced to learn as I go," Verena expressed.

"Learn as you go... do as you must. You got to do whatever it takes to keep Eric interested in you."

"I'm doing the best I could. It's just that this being pregnant shit has caused me to pick up a lot of weight. I'm not as mobile or as active as I once was. I can't be. And I've gotten older, Tiffany. I'm—"

"Forty-two going on forty-three," Tiffany cut her off to say. "I know and understand all this. But what do you plan to do, continue to make excuses, or get proactive with your man and your personal life? Remember this is something *you* started, Verena. You was the one who ditched Montell and made the choice to be with Eric. You can't fault no one but yourself for the choices you made. So, take accountability," Tiffany spoke bluntly to her friend. "And besides, you're blessed to have twins on the way at this age, girl."

"I know, and everything that glitters ain't gold either, is it. I get your point, Tiffany. I just want Eric, to get back to paying me more attention like he used to."

"Well, get back to doing the shit you used to in order to make him pay you that attention again. And since we brought up his name, Montell finally got out."

There was a pause before Verena managed to respond, "So! Why do he matter to me now?" she retorted coldly.

"Well, I'm just saying. He did not look too happy about the fact you left him the way you did. He pushed up on me and expressed himself about it before he left. He seemed to be really pissed off, Verena. Like it's going to be a serious confrontation the moment y'all encounter one another," the friend warned.

"Girl, he'll be alright. He just wasn't what I wanted in a man. I got turned off by him. I couldn't see myself being heavily involved with a guy I once had power over and told what *dafuq* to do. And Eric was refreshing for me. More charming. Also, he was free. So that's why I ended up going in the direction I did in being with him over Montell." She had finally confessed and let Tiffany know.

"So, Verena, why didn't you just *tell* Montell what the deal was in the beginning, and clearly spell it out for him, all you wanted it to be, long before y'all got deep the way y'all did?"

"Because I didn't feel the need to explain myself to an *inmate! Dafuq!* And I wasn't going to explain *anything,* to an inmate either. But then, Montell delivered. He backed up all that big talk, by making money. That changed the landscape between us. It made me look at him different. I respected him more. But I never truly liked him."

"So why did you give into him and had sex with him as y'all did? That's taking a major chance with your freedom, wasn't it?"

"Because I had felt it to be appropriate to at least give Montell some once or twice, for all the money he had produced for me. Besides, sex was all I figured he had wanted and not a relationship. Since he didn't seem to have the patience to wait until he got out to get it. And him pressuring me the way he did. I don't think that was a bad bargain though. Me and my body twice, for fifteen minutes each time, for almost a million and a half dollars of scam money I helped him to get. It was my money all along, because if it wasn't for me, providing him those names and those phones, he wouldn't have never been in position to begin with, to process the information, and get the returns he had," Verena explained. She then got on Tiffany's ass. "And why you got so many damn questions and so many concerns about Montell anyway, *Tiffany*?!" Verena spat, in a bit of an angry tone now.

***

The conversation continued. "Well, if you must know, the reason why I have so many questions and seem to be so concerned is because I detected something very alarming in that boy's words and his demeanor. He is a mad man, Verena. It scared me in a way."

"*Psss!* Montell ain't gone do nothing but go out and find someone else to manipulate and possibly land back in prison. He's a good dude overall, don't get me wrong. He just wasn't someone *I* could've seen myself with, and didn't have what it was *I* was looking for in a man. I'm glad you let me know though."

One last question on Montell, Verena, and that'll be it."

"What?"

"Do you think he's more angry at the fact you took all the money and left him. Or, more so mad because you chose to be with Eric, his *friend*, over him?"

"Hmm, I believe he's mad at the fact I ended up with Eric, and not him. But here's the thing. I *never* told Montell I was with Eric. And I never told him that I was his lady, or that we would be together once he got free. Not if I remember correctly. But I may had. And if I did, it was only something to make him feel good and to do more work, and not snitch us out. Besides, he was the one who developed the wrong impression. I didn't give him reason to believe like this in no type of way."

"Well, I'm sure it wasn't hard for him to figure out you and Eric got together. And maybe you didn't give him proper clarity."

"Well, whatever the case may had been, he get the picture now."

"I just knew it was important to at least let you know. That's all."

"And I thank you, Tiff. But how is everything going at the Home Depot job you got?" Verena changed the subject in asking.

"Everything good. It pays very well. Things would've been ten times more profitable for me though, had we started the business *you* and I had always talked about and had planned to do. What happened to that?"

"What happened to that was, I got pregnant, Tiffany. With these damn twins. But everything still in progress, boo boo. I promise you. Just let me have my babies first and get situated. Then, we gone proceed as planned. And I did give your ass $50,000, didn't I?"

"You did that."

"I know *dafuq* I did too!" Verena proclaimed. "But anyway, when you plan on coming up to visit us?"

"It won't be too much longer. Definitely before you have the baby shower, and then again, for the baby shower itself, possibly. You know I got to be there for you to have my God-babies, Eric Jr and Erika. I'm probably more excited than you are, 'Rena."

Girl, I'm just so happy to finally have the opportunity to be a mother. It's taken its toll on me. But it's worth it."

I know what you mean, boo boo. I know what you mean." The phone call between the two lasted maybe thirty more minutes, as they had a few other things to catch up on.

Tiffany had gotten all the answers from her friend about how she thought and felt towards Montell. Tiffany was absolutely attracted to Montell and wanted to explore the opportunity for both of them to get to know each other on a deeper level. She didn't like the way Verena had done the boy and felt the need to right the wrongs of her longtime friend, by providing a level of comfort and security to the mind and the heart of Montell. Verena had made some key points on what it was she had with Montell.

But where the problem lay was in the fact that, she allowed him to be led on and wasn't clear on things. Then she took a liking to his friend, which she had a right to do, but went foul by running off with the money and not leaving him any of it. But that was a time long passed. And she had a life with Eric now, and wanted to make the best of it.

He was still down in the basement sipping on bubbly and watching videos and clips from The Breakfast Club when Verena eased down to check on him and attempt to sweet talk dude back to bed.

"You still not able to rest yet, sweetie?" Verena asked to initiate a conversation with him.

"Nah. Not quite yet, baby. My mind been running non-stop on the business side of things." He responded to Verena, as she walked up to kiss him then wrapped her arms around his waist for a hug.

"So, what's on your mind, baby? Talk to me," She encouraged him.

"Oh, it's nothing too much. I'm still trying to process everything...the you and I thing...the twins...the trip from the south to the north away from everybody I knew, to begin a new life. I feel good in a way, and then, I feel bad. Because of how Montell got caught up between," Eric related.

Verena jarred her at the mention of dude's name for a second time she'd heard it that night.

She let out, "How did Montell become part of your thoughts?" She wanted to know.

"Me, Montell, and the boys, has great history together, and shared a bond like no other. We were close. I got a call from my mom, and she told me he's out and came by the house, hoping to get in touch with me. She already knew not to give out my information to no one without my permission first. I had to tell her to not ever give him any of my information. And to tell him next time he comes by, she don't think it's a good idea for him to stop by unannounced anymore, and that I don't want him to have my number. I had to have my mom do my dirty work for *me*. Ain't that a bitch!"

"Eric, you make me feel like you no longer happy with me. Like you've grown tired of what we got going on." Verena put it out there for him to respond to.

"It's not that, Verena. It's not. I just feel like I did some bullshit, some slimy low-down bullshit. And crossed out my homie, to have you. I betrayed a friend, Verena. I broke the code of loyalty. I pulled some slimy shit! And that shit ain't cool. By no means," Eric said. Now feeling the brunt of regret over his actions.

Whether or not Verena knew it, the regret that Eric was feeling was a real thing. He was a man of integrity. A man of respect. And a man that moved by the code. And presently, he felt that he'd violated his very on code of principles. The platform that every Man of Honor pride themselves on standing upon. And the only thing left to do from that point, was to find a way to make things right again, after having betrayed his whole team over a few dollars and a piece of pussy. Man, how weak was he. He would soon come to know.

One

Chapter 1

Verena cocked her head to the side and looked into Eric's face to try to gauge how serious he really was. She knew without a doubt, he was big on being a man of integrity, as that was one of the qualities about him she greatly respected. And she had to say something or do something, to stop him from beating himself up about the past.

"Eric. Look. Let me be perfectly clear with you, okay." Her authoritative nature kicked in. "Me and Montell, was never a couple, okay. We was never together, per se. So, let's just get that part straight first. I was never his lady, and he was never my man. What we had going on was business. Nothing more. Simple and plain. He never was who *I* wanted. And he never had what *I* wanted. That, sir, would be you. Okay. You see how fast I gave you the pussy, right?"

But Verena, if only you knew, how serious he was about you. And how much he used to speak so highly of you."

Eric, so what! All that shit doesn't even matter anymore, sweetie. It was what it was. And it is what it is. I had caught onto the game and the manipulation tactics Montell was trying to use on me. In fact, I don't know if you remember or not, but I do. Perfectly well. It was *you* who told me that Montell had been lying to me and manipulating me all along, right?"

"Yeah."

"And that it was *you,* not that nigga who made the whole money-making scheme work. That it was *you,* in your own words, who brought home the bacon and the bread. Do you remember?"

"Yeah, I recall," he replied.

"And if I'm not mistaken, it was *you*, not Montell, who turned what was to only be a twenty-minute exchange of money from your hands to mine, to a four-hour date, over a small meal and flavors of ice cream, where you filled my head with everything you wanted to and really got my attention. It was you who turned me into who I am for you. It was you who drew me to you and all you had in mind, And it was you who convinced me to no longer deal with Montell, but to get down with the program you was the captain of, right?" She spat.

"Yeah, you right sweetie."

Well then, don't give me the second guessing of choices and the decisions you made, Eric. I'm *your* woman. And I need you to get back to paying me the attention you used to. I also need *you*, to get back to giving me, the sexual attention and satisfaction you once had. I've been missing it. And I've got to have it," she made him aware of.

"Psss! That's all your ass seem to want anyway, is for us to fuck every day."

That would be nice." Verena said then pulled his head down to her level and they tongue kissed wildly.

Eric then pulled off his wife-beater. Verena kissed on his chest and licked his neck as she liked to do. As she nibbled on his pecks and tickled the tips of his nipples with her tongue, she reached down inside his sweatpants to massage his manhood to peak erection. He lowered his pants to his ankles, boxer-briefs included, and allowed his manhood to stick out long strong and ready to be taken hostage of by her.

Verena leaned down to waist level and took him into her mouth. The warmth and moisture caused him to quiver ecstatically from the sensation. He regained composure and allowed her to do work.

She started slowly, letting her lips glide down his thick imposing shaft and deep throat as much as she could, pausing momentarily, then easing back up while pulling tightly with her lips, using suction as technique, to draw the blood from the lower end of his sex organ to the head. She then tightly grabbed his dick with her right hand squeezing, causing the head to inflate double the size, then popped her full lips on it four to five times before going into rhythm. Verena bobbed up-and-down, up-and-down, up-and-down, doing all necessary to please her man.

With both hands, she jerked him off and continued to work the top portion with her mouth above the circumcision ring. Eric leaned back and propped himself on the pool table to allow full range and stretch of his meat-stick to extend to the max. All nine inches he was packing.

Verena hummed on the knob and spit on the dick, getting it sloppy and as wet as she possibly could. Eric loved when she got dirty and nasty with it. He didn't like all the professional formal shit which came along with her. He had to break her out of it.

He cupped Verena under the chin with his right hand and held the top of her head steady with his left. Then, he humped hard and fast as he could in her mouth and down her throat, causing her to gag but enjoying the thrill in the way he liked her to suck his dick. He had specifically taught her how to blow him off in the right way that would cause him grand pleasure. He was cumming, blowing a thick robust load in less than five minutes. Verena never came off the dick for air. She swallowed the whole *creme de ca cao.*

"Now come on. Let's go to the bedroom for round two. Because you ain't fucked me in over a month. And I want some bad," She directed.

"No problem, sweetie. You can have all you like. I've got to keep you lubricated and open for the babies to have it easy coming out." Eric responded, then pecked her on the forehead before pulling up his pants, grabbing his tank-top,

20

and making way from the basement to the bedroom, to put it on Verena as she wanted.

They buried all the petty misunderstandings about Montell then and there. And they put to rest Eric's moral guilt he felt. But little did Verena know, there was nothing or no one, that could slow Eric from the pursuit of the hot piece of ass the Latina sensation, Joleena, had his sights and interest set on. He had to have her. No doubt about it. Verena had competition on her hands. A stiff version of it.

***

With him being back in Atlanta, Montell, Roderick, and Jamie, became close again as they were before they got knocked and went to prison. The plan that they had in mind was to score one big take with the scamming thing again, then take all the money from it and put into the clubbing industry, maybe open a strip joint and go legit.

The bottom line was that they didn't want to continue with taking chances doing illegal things and run the risk of being indicted and going back to prison. But then again, by them being taken down and convicted before, was no fault of their own. It belonged to the friend who turned rat, Rico Locus. And the issue was still on the table with what to do about him flipping the script and crossing them out the way he had.

Also, Eric had to be served his fair share of punishment, behind the fuck shit he pulled. Because they all took an oath. And it would be 'death before dishonor,' along with the unity rule of 'bros over hoe's' on any given day of the week. So, the three amigos had to conduct *realpolitik* and discuss many things that surrounded the future of them as they remained the group they always had been without the weak links.

They met up at Jamie's place one Sunday afternoon to put things together and come up with a plan to pool their money and make something happen from a business perspective.

21

They knew it was important to get legit and to stay that way, because the Feds would always have them under their watchful eyes and never let up.

Jamie and Roderick had no knowledge about the cash and jewelry Montell stashed and his recovery of it once he got free. For all they knew, he had only the $60,000 they'd gave him, a list of names and other personal information he'd brought home from prison, and access to a near $100,000 line of credit at the bank through his mother's name and the small businesses she had success with while Montell was away. The sit down was for them to strategize and put a business plan together to propel them forward.

"So, look fellas," Jamie began. "I thought of a brilliant idea to help us profit in a major way, and put us on the path to going legit, because I ain't trying to go back to prison no more."

"Boy what you talking about, my nigga!" Montell chimed in to cosign.

"I figured before long we would finally get our shit together and put money in a positive direction," said Roderick.

"But here is the deal. I think we could put one more lick together from the names and information Montell got for us. Then, take all the money and invest into something I think we all can agree upon," Jamie suggested.

"And what might that be?" Montell asked.

"Bitches...dance moves...and top dollar alcohol to drink," Jamie revealed.

"So, a strip club is what you got in mind, huh?" Roderick asked.

"You damn right, it is. How could we go wrong? There's never a shortage in demand for either," Jamie added.

"It sounds like something I could get interested in," Montell stated.

"We just need to hit another lick and get the type of money necessary to get a good start in this line of business.

Because here in ATL, we got some stiff competition we gone be up against. So, once we get it going, we gonna need to come up with creative ways to keep people interested in what we got to offer, over everybody else," Montell suggested.

"Here is something I wanna put out there. How about we tie in with somebody who already owns a bar or some small club, and who's looking to expand? We get familiar with how this shit go through them, because it ain't no way in all hell anyone of us here, gone be able to get the city council members to grant us a liquor license. We all just got out the fucking Feds and we convicted felons. Not to mention, we *niggaz* at that! Which means, it's gone be much harder," Roderick brought them to reality.

"Yeah, you right, Rod. It would be a wise thing to tie in with somebody who already know the business. But who?" Jamie remarked and asked.

"I got a nigga in mind for that. I could push up on him and see what the lick read," Montell answered up. "Such a transition from a bar to a club. Girls gone be wide open in there. That may bring along too many additional problems and cause too much unwanted attention by the feds again. Instead of the IRS, we'll have to then worry about the ATF and the DEA," Montell stated.

"Not if we legit. We ain't got to worry about them, if we getting money in the right way," Roderick said.

"Yeah, that's true. But both of you know just the well as I do, with the success of one business, it can open the door for success in something else. And whatever I got to do to make it and be successful and take care of my kids, then that's what I'll do," Jamie made it known from his point of view.

"First things first, let's just get this muthafuckin' money! Then, we could go from there. And if we have to get gangsta and rock a few heads or two, then its whatever. I'm with the bullshit. I want all the smoke. I'm from Philly, baby. We 'bout that life!' And sometimes, niggaz gotta make statements in order to gain the respect necessary to make it in the game. So, if it's the clubbing industry y'all niggaz wanna move into, or a high-powered sports bar, then that's what it is. Let's get to it and stop bullshitting," Roderick asserted.

"But onto the next subject. What y'all feel need to go down about the fuck shit the nigga Eric pulled? In my opinion, the nigga crossed all us out. The whole team," Montell stated.

"I can't say, Montell. What do *you* feel need to go down? Since it was you who the nigga got down on? You know the nigga ain't gonna give you back no bread. And you know the nigga don't intend to turn the bitch loose. So, what you feel like need to happen?" Jamie stated and demanded to know.

"Man, that nigga disgraced us! He crossed all us out. But this shit more personal than anything. I've got a trick for they...Eric and Verena. Because revenge is a dish best served cold. And I got ice running through my muthafuckin' veins, yo. Real talk!" Montell responded.

***

They talked on. "Whatever you do nigga, just be careful. And don't bring no heat back to the table. Truth be told, everything the nigga did, is worthy of death! Me personally, I'll have the nigga taken care of first, if I come across him before you do," Roderick stated.

"Yeah, that's fucked up on E's behalf. The type of money he ran off with, got the power to get a whole fucking family knocked off! Not to mention the other shit. But just do what you gotta do, bruh. The nigga deserve it," Jamie further instigated.

"But anyway, back to this club thing. You came up with a name for it yet?" Roderick asked, looking in Jamie and Montell's direction.

"Actually, I do," Jamie responded.

24

"What?" Roderick and Montell asked at the same time and had to knock on the wooden table afterwards.

"'Passion City' or 'Club Passion.' Which one sound more appealing to y'all?" Jamie wanted to know.

"I like Club Passion," said Montell.

"So do I," mentioned Roderick, piggy-backing on Montell.

"That's exactly the one I had in mind, since Atlanta already got a 'Magic City.' We don't need too many strip clubs with 'city' to it being tossed out there. It may cause a confusion between the two. So, 'Club Passion' it is, my niggaz. I'll go ahead and get a logo designed and copyright the name to get us started," Jamie said.

"That's what's up my nigga." Montell said, and the trio continued on talking over a multitude of things.

Montell tried to simmer down and keep a level head about the whole Eric and Verena situation. But his anger wouldn't allow him to. He had vengeance on his mind and blood in his eyes. He'd been disrespected to the ultimate degree. And those two conniving disrespectful motherfuckers, has to pay the piper! He only needed to locate them, then take action. That was it.

***

Montell made it his business to head to the DMV and have his driver's license reinstated. He then had his mom drive to Atlanta, and they went to the car dealership to buy him a ride. He selected one of the new model Infiniti SUV's, black in color with the cream interior. It was a one owner certified vehicle, previously driven by an older white guy who never traveled much. It only had 3000 miles on it, and Montell had his mother finance it for him with a $25,000 deposit. He was good to go from that point.

He'd maintained contact with Tamron and had also reconnected with his white girlfriend he'd dealt with before going to prison. This was Mandy, Mandy Barfield. She had a job as a bank teller and was doing pretty good for herself. Mandy had come a long way from the job she had while in college working at Circle K. Once she graduated, she moved on up in the world, but still, had time for her guy Montell, the one who gave her the first interracial sexual experience.

She wanted her and Montell to go out on a date, something he would definitely be up to with her, being he now had time to entertain, unlike the years between college and his arrest, when they'd only got together every so often, but enjoyable moments they were.

She called him on a Saturday afternoon. The time was about 2:00 P.M. "Hey! How you doing, Mandy," he answered.

"I'm well, Montell. And you?" she responded.

"Life is grand baby. It's grand," he said while staring in to the lens of the camera as they video chat on Messenger.

"You still have a handsome smile about yourself, don't you," Mandy complimented as it was the first time they'd video called and saw one another since he'd been free.

"I'm still me, baby. Just a new and improved version I know you will absolutely love," he said.

"Is that right?" she responded.

"That's a fact, sweetie."

"So, what you got going on later this evening?"

I don't have too much lined up. Why, what's good?" he wanted to know.

"Oh, nothing too much. I just thought it would be nice, if you and I could go out some place, and enjoy for a little while," she said.

"Sounds all right to me. You know I got time for you. Don't forget, it was you Mandy who held me down and supported me while I was in prison. So, if anything, I do owe you a debt of gratitude," he stated.

"You're fine, baby. I held you down and supported you because it was what I was supposed to have done as your girlfriend. Until you insisted I go on about life and not hold up on you. But you're home now, and I'm not with no one. And I would like for us to get on the path to being a couple again. Because I'm desperate to know what this 'new and improved' version of Montell Jermaine McNeal, is talking about, and is all about," Mandy addressed him by his full government name.

"Well, don't you worry, Mandy Allison Barfield. You'll definitely have your fair share of my time now. What time best for you today?" he asked.

"About six will be fine. I'll pick you up. Just text me your address. Where would you like to go?"

I've seen so many of those Buffalo Wild Wings commercials and ads, I've got to check one out. It looks like an exciting and fun spot to visit," he stated.

"Buffalo Wild Wings and a movie it is then, suga. I'll see you at six," she let him know.

"Okay. See you later, alligator," he replied.

"After while, crocodile," she replied. They ended the call.

He had fallen back to sleep for another hour or two before getting up and began to get prepared for his night out on the town with Mandy, his lovely "pink-toe." Montell took a shower and shaved his head as always, to perfection while under the hot steamy water. Then, he lined the full thick beard of his to a razor-sharp liking. He got dressed in one of his Jordan sweatsuits and put on a freshly bought pair of Retro Air Jordan's, the Space Jams Bugs Bunny joints, as the sweatsuit had matched the colors to perfection.

While in prison, Montell managed to find himself conscience-wise and culture-wise. He thoroughly studied, then joined up with some cats out of New York City and New Jersey. In particular, some dudes from the Bronx and Trenton, who he'd gotten his enlightenment from.

He'd became a member of The Nation of Gods and Earths and declared himself a "Five-Percenter" or "God-Body," so to speak, and applied the "Book of Life" the 120 lessons, the

Supreme Mathematics, and Supreme Alphabet to his way of thinking and daily life. All this occurred while in the Federal system. But for the most part, he only proved to be a walking contradiction, representing NGE and dating a white girl.

Chapter 2

The influence of The Nation of Gods and Earths had come about from the dudes he was around and through the profound and esoteric nature of the lessons Montell studied. Also, from the images he saw online of heavily famous people he greatly respected who were Five-Percenters themselves and wore articles of the Nation to prove it. Most notably, Jay Z, with the thick and heavily weighted gold chain and medallion of the Universal Flag of the Nation he'd donned for all to see and know what he represented.

But at the same time, Montell, semi contradicted what he claimed to stand upon, by embracing a Caucasian female, more so than a Sister. Albeit, this was subject to change. *Everything* is made new over time. Even the things that's deeply held dear.

Montell himself, bought a nice sized Cuban link chain that was about twenty-four to twenty-six inches long and three quarters of an inch wide. The custom designed medallion of the Universal Flag of NGE was a quarter of an inch thick, about the size in diameter of the lid that goes on the top of an eight-ounce Styrofoam cup. In addition, he had on a top dollar Casio G-Shock watch Tamron gave him as a welcome home gift. To complete the outfit, he last dabbed on grade A quality body oil to please the soul and to beautify the atmosphere. His fragrance of choice was Jimmy Choo for men.

Montell examined himself in the full-length mirror. He posed from side-to-side and from other angles in admiration of his presence. Dude definitely loved all he saw. He lastly talked to himself as he marveled at the image the mirror projected. His cellphone rang, snapping him out of the fascinating moment he briefly experienced. It was Mandy. She was out front of the apartment waiting to pick him up.

He made his way to her SUV. Mandy owned a new model BMW X5. Montell hopped in, kissed his sexy "snow bunny," and they rode off, en route to the nearest Buffalo Wild Wings to enjoy the great food they have to offer.

Montell ordered a variety of flavorful seasoned wings with a large order of steak fries, while Mandy opted for her favorite, mild wings, blue cheese dressing, and carrot and celery sticks. They devoured their meals, and took delight in the sports atmosphere the crowd was made up of, as they were all entertained by the multiple TV monitors that surrounded the place and held a decent conversation to catch up on a few things.

They left there and went to the movie theater at Lenox Square Mall. The movie Montell mostly wanted to see was something that was loaded with crime drama, or a thriller even. Something similar to "Motherless Brooklyn." He loved that movie. It was a new age mob film that was sure to satisfy with the story line. He favored these style of drama shows. Motherless Brooklyn was of course pre-pandemic.

They left the movies and went to Montell's place to relax and talk more. "So, Mandy, did you miss me while I was gone, baby?" Montell initiated.

"Of course. You know I missed you, Montell. I tried to stay down with you, but you didn't want me to. So, what was a gal to do?" she replied.

"I definitely do appreciate those visits and money you looked out for me with."

"No pressure babe. No pressure."

"But anyways, what happen with you and the guy you mentioned to me you'd began dealing with?"

You're talking about Dylan?"

"Yeah. That's his name. Dylan."

We was together for about three years, then, his alcohol consumption and Meth addiction had gotten the best of him. He had begun to steal from me, Montell. He stole from his parents. And began committing petty crimes to support the drug habit. I called it off with him and never said anything more. Last I heard, he was in and out of rehab trying to get himself together. I've dated since me and him, but nothing serious. I know I don't even have to ask about you of your dealings, with the plethora of females you once seemed to preoccupy yourself with?" Mandy stated, with a pinch of sarcasm and curiosity to her words.

"Yeah, but I still made time for my favorite white chick, Mandy A. Barfield." Montell came back with, causing her to smile and blush like no other behind his remark. "You still hang out with your girls...Abby, Chelsea, Donna, and Amanda?"

"Of course, I do. Abby and Donna married now and got kids. They don't really have time to do much of anything. And Amanda moved away to Arizona. She come home every now and then. But Chelsea and I still do a lot of things together."

"What about your parents? They still find themselves opposed to you having dealings with a 'black guy?' They still stuck in the days of the 'old south' in the 'New Millennium?" he wanted to know.

"My dad still has his ways. But my mom is far more accepting in now day and time. She says as long as I'm happy, it's fine by her. Especially so, since things fell to hell with Dylan and I. They don't know anything about you being incarcerated."

"Oh, they don't?"

"Nope."

"And the white guy you dated for three years, it all went to hell, you say?" Montell sarcastically remarked.

"Yep. The white guy I dated for three years, if that makes you feel better to hear me say," Mandy said reluctantly.

"You good. But check this out, sweetie. Here is the good part about it all. Now is the best opportunity more so than ever, for us to have all we've wanted together as a couple," he propositioned.

"Montell, you know you don't want nothing to do with me full time. I'm just a plain ole' bland ole' white girl, and a hopeless romantic at best. Besides, I'm too caught up in my career at the bank for anything. What do you want with me?"

Baby, you best believe, I got what it takes to pipe you up a little, darling. I can put some soul in your life, girl."

"Oh really! You got what it takes to 'pipe' me up, huh? And add some soul to my life?"

"I had what it took in times before, didn't I?"

Yeah, you did. I just wanted more of your time. But you didn't have none for me."

"You want to know why, Mandy?" He asked while eyeing her seriously as they sat and watched music videos on YouTube.

"Yeah, why?"

"It's because I really liked you, and didn't want to do you wrong. That's why. I spared you, Mandy. I really did."

"Oh. You don't say. So, you finally speak on how you felt, after all these years Montell," Mandy remarked.

"Can't say you don't know now. But come here. With your little sexy smart-ass." He said and pulled her close to him, then immediately began to ravish her with kisses all about the neck, lips, and cleavage area wildly. In an alpha-male type way. Just how Mandy liked him to take advantage of her.

***

They began to tongue-kiss then Montell took to task of getting Mandy out of her clothes by helping pull her shirt over her head and removing the bra, allowing those 34C cup breast to be fully exposed and jiggle enticingly. Montell had already removed his top, his chain, and relaxed in a solid white tank top.

Mandy lay back on the sofa topless and stretched her legs for Montell to remove her pants after he'd taken off the casual boots she wore. Baby girl had on a pair of pink laced panties. She eased them off from under her 36-inch hips, ass, and thighs. Mandy was a gymnast, so she'd always maintained a fit figure. Before the day, she'd visited a tanning salon, and her skin was balanced in tone and ideal for the eye candy she gave Montell. The temperature of the living room was at a comfortable level. A diverse blend of music videos played on the TV and the mood was set just right.

Montell got completely naked, then sat between Mandy's legs on the sofa. "I'm about to drive your ass crazy, shawdy. You hear me."

"Talk is cheap. And I'm not a prepaid Metro wireless. So, show me what you talking about," she came back with.

He next buried his face in her love-box, as he'd gotten a whiff of her vaginal aroma and wanted to taste her love. Mandy raised her legs high in the air in a "V" shape, palmed Montell's head with both hands, and eagerly welcomed him into her passion zone.

He slurped on her clit and licked pleasantly between her pussy lips, causing Mandy to have an orgasm and shutter uncontrollably as the result. He next flipped her over onto her belly and had her to place a pillow underneath to cause her backside to protrude further.

Montell mounted her and sat atop her butt and hind legs. He teased by taking his right middle finger and inserting it into the pussy, sliding in and out, then rapidly tickling, pulling out, penetrating her anus, and slapping her hard on the ass; culminating different moves of foreplay to stimulate they to the max.

With no further delays, Montell slapped his manhood between her ass cheeks three to four times to take her off guard of what was to come.

"You ready for this?" he whispered into her ear.

"And you know I am. Been waiting since before you got locked up. After we last got to it."

He situated the head of his dick at the entrance of her love box and penetrated, filling her hole with the girth of his meat. Montell began to stroke slowly and passionately, developing his rhythm as he go. He picked up the pace and began to fuck Mandy real thorough.

Each time his balls slapped against those rosy ass cheeks of hers, it sent shock waves of pleasure and sensation shooting throughout her body. It was as if she was being electrocuted or some sort. It felt so damn good to her. She had to bite down on one of the pillows to keep from bellowing like a female moose while breeding out in the wild.

Montell always gave Mandy the dick bareback, as they never used a condom. She loved to feel him raw, and he loved to release his load all over her face and breast each time he ejaculated. But this time would be different. A much ecstatic scenario. He'd tightened his grip around her waist and began to thrust himself harder and faster. Then, all of a sudden, he locked her waist excessively and planted firm while remaining hung deep inside. His pelvic was flush against her ass cheeks and the lips of her pussy.

Montell had reached his climax. He exploded every milliliter of his load in her love pool. He grunted and growled as he felt the burn of satisfaction from the pungent fire that cumming deep within a piece of forbidden fruit could only produce. Mandy felt Montell's seed flooding her womb. He was backed up beyond imagination. It was the second piece of pussy he'd gotten since being free. He'd had already fucked and his dick sucked twice before the day. By

Tamron, and another time by a prostitute he'd met in Albany who had enticed him.

Montell didn't even withdraw his dick from Mandy. He just remained hung deep and laid on her back, panting and breathing hard, like he'd just ended running from the police following a high-speed chase.

"Damn Mandy. This pussy still great to me," he reminded.

"And you still got the magic touch babe. Keep fucking me please. I need it in my life. This chocolate and sweet dick of yours. You did say you was gonna pipe me up, right? Keep going. Pipe me up, then," Mandy replied.

Still hard and built to continue, Montell began pumping slowly, as they went for round two. They loved it. They couldn't get enough of the other.

***

Jamie had gotten aggressive in his pursuit to secure a veteran business partner to help them get things going on what they had in mind. He needed someone who already owned a mediocre bar or club and was looking to expand or make significant progress at some point with an additional installment.

This would be a grand opening of a premiere gentleman's club for me and the boys. The likes Atlanta had never seen before, thought Jamie.

Being that Jamie was originally from Jacksonville Florida and had adopted ATL as his home now, he had somewhat of a hard time linking up with any old-school business minded principled dude. Someone who he felt was ideal, and who he could convince to invest in the vision and plan that he had in his head. Of them all, it was he who was most determined. But nobody really knew Jamie like that, and this hindered the process.

However, all had changed at the point of him visiting one of his old haunts on the west side of the city and holding a deep conversation with the owner of a small bar, a cat named Felix Spencer.

He had a *tittie* joint near the Bankhead section of town that made just enough money to keep food on his table, his bills paid, gas in his Cadillac, his woman happy, and the bar operating properly. Jamie used to love spending time in such a low-key spot when sipping on suds, downing a few shots of *Henny*, talking shit with the fellas, and being entertained by the girls. All of this occurred during his days in college and prior to him going to the feds.

He and ol' Felix developed a relationship by Jamie selling him multiple cases of beer, liquor, and cigarettes on many occasions at a discount to supply the bar. Jamie and his guys bought up much as they could at any time the supply was available on the black market from other outlaw enterprises who hijacked cargo trucks, broke into package stores, or burglarized supply warehouses. Eric was the only one from their crew who picked up where he left off on this end once he'd gotten free. But Jamie and Roderick were still open to it. Montell probably would be as well, once he was to finally reveal what it was he wanted to get involved in.

Chapter 3

Felix, was a sixty-seven-year-old retired pimp, who married his last standing hoe, Melange aka "Pepper." He had an elder brother who was in the pimp business himself for many years, before letting it go and eventually getting arrested, and being sentenced to life in the Georgia penal system for a cold case homicide of an undercover police back in 1975. Felix's brother name is Terry, but his moniker was "Pimp TJ" Terry Jackson his government.

Felix went *by "Pimp Rolex,"* behind his fond love and infatuation of the quality brand watchmaker, and him being famous for always stating, *"bitch, you know what time it is!"* Or one of his other phrases, *"Never tick or tok, bitch! Continue to keep it moving!"* The message he conveyed to his girls was to *"Never get mad at a trick"* and *"Don't stay in one spot too long, or don't spend too much time on the job."* Pimp philosophy property applied in real time.

Jamie pulled up on Felix about a week after he, Roderick, and Montell held their conversation about opening a club. Felix was in the back of his joint, hosting *a "Skins"* card game. But he still had the time to chop it up with anybody about potential business.

"What's good, young playa," Felix greeted Jamie. "How you been, dude?"

"It's been good for me, you know. It's been good, Felix."

"When you made it back out here to the real world? How long you been home now?"

"I been out for a few months. Probably right at a year. And man, don't it feel good to be free." Jamie said and smiled as he and Felix took a seat in a room next to the one the card game was going on at, to have their private discussion.

"So, you say you been out probably just at a year now, huh? But what I don't understand is what the hell took you so long to swing by Ponytails, to give ol' Felix here a holla? I thought we was better than that?"

"We are, Felix. And I had every intent in the world to pay you your due respect. But I been home back in J-Ville, and just recently got back to the A," Jamie lied.

"Oh okay. I was about to say. I know we better than that. But what's on ya mind though, Young'n? And to be a young nigga, you always had grown folks business to bring my way." Felix encouraged him to get on about the business he wanted to discuss.

Jamie was thirty-nine. At the time he'd began doing business with Felix, he was twenty-seven.

"Felix, look. You know me and my boys ain't never brought no bullshit your way, right."

"Right. I know."

"Okay. So, here is what we got in mind. We got about a hundred to a hundred fifty thousand between the three of us. And we would like to partner up with you to open up a gentleman's lounge, right here in the city of our own," he revealed.

"You say, you and your two guys, got between a hundred to a hundred-fifty large ones, and you looking to partner up with me on and open up a gentleman's lounge here in Atlanta?" the old man retorted.

"'That's right, big time. We looking to link up with you and do some next level shit," Jamie responded by speaking with both his mouth and his hands.

"What's the 'catch twenty-two' behind this? It's more to it, I'm sure. Out of all these people here in Atlanta, why me?" he definitely wanted to know.

"Out of all the people in the A-Town, why *not* you, Felix? That's the better question."

"Break it down for me. I'm listening."

You see, look Felix, '*unc*,'" Jamie attached with a smile. "We already got a solid business relationship from times in the past."

"Right," Felix injected and nodded his head three times in agreement.

"And I remember times in the past how you used to speak about keeping this place also having a bigger space some day for your girls to bring in more money. You remember that, right?"

You got a good memory don't you, young blood." Felix was charmed by Jamie's quotes of him.

"I do. But anyway, you know we don't deal with no dope. So, we ain't got to worry about any extra attention from 'the man,'" Jamie went old school with his terminology to appeal to the spirit of ol' Felix and cause him to *feel* where he was coming from. "We looking to take our money and stay legit. We can lease a building, renovate it to fit the theme and the atmosphere of a gentleman's lounge, have nothing but the best doing their thing, and entice nothing but a respectable, mature, and high-profile clientele up in the piece to be entertained," he proposed.

"What about the alcohol?" Felix wanted to know "Ain't no such thing as girls and entertainment without no drinks!"

"And *that's* the main part I was getting at. You the one who's gonna fulfill that area. The reason why I came to you is because we've done outstanding business in the past on vice your spot legitimately sells. And you got the license to keep the drinks flowing and the cups full, my guy. I'm sure you got a steady connection down at City Hall with those council members who you can grease the palms of heavily with 'Blue Cheese,' at our expense, and get them to enhance the amount of alcohol you're able to sell on the license you already got, right?"

"I *might* be able to do a little something. It depends on how much we talking, and on what percentage I get out the club thing, *if* I decide to get on board," Felix stated emphatically.

"What percent you had in mind?"

"I ain't necessarily had no percentage in mind. But now, you've gave me a brighter future to look forward to. It's a pleasure to know y'all want to go in business with Felix and his people." He said, displaying a wide smile, like he'd been granted a clemency from death row or a "stay of execution" to halt being terminated.

"So, I take your positive reaction as a *yes*, you in on what we got in mind to do?" Jamie sought clarity.

"It's a strong possibility my guy. A strong possibility. Besides, in now day and times, it seems like the most popular clubs in Atlanta, are those fuckin' *gay* spots that seem to keep poppin' up every damn where! Like the goddamn *Bulldog* over in Zone Three Mechanicsville! We got to get people back into the natural habit of seduction and attraction in the A-Town. The tradition this city is historically known for, long before the 'Freak Nik' and all the above." Felix made a valid point and stated exactly why he would more than likely get involved.

Chapter 4

Felix's experience as an ex-pimp and a man who was absolutely obsessed with the culture and the lifestyle surrounding anything on such level, wouldn't allow this opportunity to go in vain. To him, a strip club is a modified and far more improved platform to work from. An extension of the pimp game itself, if you will. Felix never stated that he was, in fact, *done* with the game *completely*. He only declared himself *retired* from pimping. But niggaz come out of retirement all the time in many fields, and there was plenty of money still to be made. Especially so for Felix, since he didn't have to put up none of his own funds to make things pop. Just simply make wise decisions and properly advise Jamie and crew on theirs.

"So, it's three of y'all and one of me, right?"

"Sho' your right."

"One hundred divided by four, twenty-five percent, right? Plus, my license. Plus, my connections at city hall and with the mayor, right?"

"Right."

"Okay. I need thirty-five percent of everything, and y'all split the remainder. Of course, I know this will occur once we pay off everybody on our payroll."

"You absolutely right on everything, Felix. I feel you deserve the additional ten percent for all you gonna bring to the table. Is that what you want?" Jamie was looking to close the deal.

"Yeah, that's *exactly* what I want," Felix said and stretched out his hand to shake Jamie's.

"That's a bet. I'll have a lawyer draw up the contract and be sure to have all the details highlighted within. And once this is done, we could go from there. But in the meantime, here," Jamie said and pulled out a roll of money. He peeled off ten $100 bills and gave it to Felix. "I know time is money and money is time, Felix. That's for you taking out your time to speak with me at your place," Jamie complimented with a genuine gesture.

"You see, I like how you do's business already, Young-blood. You my kind of guy. Now let's get our girls and get to the money, *playa!*" Felix said and rubbed his hands together while smiling and visualizing how sweet business is going to be.

***

Meanwhile...

Tiffany and her daughter Chasity were out doing a little shopping at Greenbrier Mall, looking for special gifts they could give to Verena, once they got up north to visit and again, to attend the baby shower. Chasity was home on break from college at Florida State University. She and her mother always enjoyed the company of one another.

Tiffany's cellphone rang. She observed the number on the caller ID. She looked at Chasity to make a determination if or not she was truly ready to make something known to her, as never before. She'd decided against this at the present time, due to not being in the right setting to do so. Putting her Bluetooth earpiece in, she then answered the phone. "Hello!"

"You have a collect call from a Federal inmate....Justin Manderville. To accept—"

BEEP!

Tiffany wasted no time with the prompt, as she'd done this on way too many occasions through the years to count.

"Hello," she answered.

"Hey, Tiffany. How are you?"

"I'm making it. I'm making it. And yourself?"

"I've just been busy back and forth, in and out of the law library here. I got this one guy whose been helping me out a lot. We trying to get some of this time reduced and as many as those wrongful convictions tossed out as possible. I at least want to get out and have a second chance at life, before I get called home. I'm getting up in age now, I'm almost fifty. And as you know, I was falsely accused of the things I'm in prison for."

"I'm aware. I've been knowing you ever since I was fifteen...sixteen years of age myself. And I do hope you would someday make it out. I don't know the facts of your cases or the legality of them, but I can honestly say you don't deserve to spend the *rest* of your life in there. It's not like you was a serial killer of some sort," Tiffany expressed.

"And I thank you for not being judgmental of me and for your support."

"Chasity's home on break again."

"Oh, she is."

"Yeah. We together now at the mall doing a little shopping. Verena due in the next months with her twins. We going to New Jersey to visit for the baby shower and to spend time with her."

"I remember you told me about Verena being pregnant and all. Ol' Verena. I remember her really well. The both of you was close then. Y'all was like sisters. What, she took a job up north in Jersey as a warden or something?"

"No. She's no longer into corrections. Her and her dude bought a house up there, and they looking to start a business or so once she drops her load and get back to moving around again. It's a long story on those two."

"It sounds that way, but on to something else. Look, Chasity a grown woman now. And I'm sure she will be able to handle the truth of all we got to tell her. When do you plan on letting her know, so we can finally move on past this long-awaited conversation and reality we've got to bring to her attention?" Justin wanted to know. "I can't die without my daughter not knowing anything about who her *true* father is."

"Justin, this has been a lot of pressure on me since day one. And I'm just as ready as you are, to finally speak our truth and get it over with. But I promise you, once I get this divorce finalized and me and my husband are no more, then, me and Chasity will make it our business to come visit you, and all three of us could sit, talk, and put it all out there, okay. I just can't right now. It will greatly alter and complicate things in the court."

"So, how you gonna convince her to fill out the paperwork and come to the prison with you? What you plan to tell her?"

"I'll come up with something, until we get inside. I've already lied to my daughter enough, and my consciousness has not allowed me any rest on no level mentally or morally. And another thing. I don't know what kind of backlash or repercussions this revelation is subject to bring, from him or her."

"What has to be done has to be done, Tiff. We can't continue to go on this way. Not like this."

"And we not. But look, let me go ahead and finish shopping, get on back home, and prepare for work tomorrow. I'll put a few dollars on your account by the end of the week and send you a brief email. I've got to go, okay. You take care," she lastly stated.

"You, too."

They concluded the call.

Tiffany had never cut off her contact with Justin through the many years he'd been locked away in prison. She couldn't, even if she tried her hardest to. The truth of their

44

acquaintance, opposite the fact Justin was secretly the father of her daughter and not the husband's, the one who assumed he was, Tiffany was still in love with Justin, and had been, ever since the day, twenty plus years ago when he took her virginity and attached himself to her in such a powerful and emotional way.

***

No matter how hard a woman tries, or what age they are, they will never forget the guy who was their first, how he made them feel at the time while in the act of sex, or the place where they were when it all went down. Tiffany was definitely not the one to lose the intensely strong emotions and feelings she held dear to as it related to Justin. Each time she looked at Chasity or hear her or Justin's voice over the phone, she's instantly reminded of her first love still being alive and needing her to continue in support. *If only it was two people who knew of this dark secret, and not four or five, then everything would be fine and dandy, she thought.* But the reality of the situation was serious.

***

Montell, Jamie, and Roderick, all huddled up again at Montell's apartment to begin the preparation and the work necessary to perfect another tax scams and other white-collar schemes to con the government out of more money. They had the proper equipment in devices, software, and all other technological material to make it do what it do. Montell had produced the pages of names and personal information of 1000 inmates who would know not one thing of their identity being stolen, or, of the monetary benefit the three of them were subject to receive, once the process was completed.

Jamie and Roderick had the list of companies that would be used, the addresses to those companies, and the Employer

Identification Numbers. They had everything at their disposal and were ready to roll, just like the last time they put together a lick. Except it appeared Jamie had begun to exert himself to the forefront, and make himself the leader, and not allow Montell the opportunity to be any longer. This could possibly cause another debacle, or entertain the prospect of being the reason why the team would suffer an additional splintering off, as was the situation between he, Eric, and the "Warden bitch!" so thought Jamie.

It was the middle of September, and they had roughly thirty days or so before the filing deadline for late submissions before year's end.

Jamie schooled Montell, "So here's how the new tax thing works out here now. Me and Rod gonna show you how it go. At least the stuff you don't know about already. A lot of shit done changed, my nigga, since we last put in some work on this tax movement. But the main thing is, we pick through the list you got there," he pointed, "and use nothing but the names and info of dudes who absolutely has no work history, same as before and are between the ages of twenty to twenty-five or twenty-nine. Then, unlike the previous numbers we aimed for between five to seven stacks, we gonna lower it to three to four, so not to raise any suspicions or throw red flags, that would cause them to be alarmed at such high numbers for a bunch of muthafuckas' who ain't got no work history. Also, out of all the names, we only gonna process three hundred, and hold back on the rest, if shit don't go right. We can try again next year." Jamie made it known how they were to operate from that point forward.

Montell had other agendas that he would perpetuate on the side. He had it in mind to process about a hundred of those names and information to benefit himself, once he was able to steal the information of those companies from Jamie, and prepare claims of his "clients" with it

Knock-Knock-Knock-Knock-Knock!

Someone was at the door. "Yo, who is it?" Montell called out.

"It's me...Mandy," she answered.

"Oh Shit. Damn, I forgot. I told my girl to drop by at this time to bring us some pizza and wings and shit, y'all," Montell said to his boys. They were hungry as ever too, as they all had smoked on some of the last gas pack the city had to offer at the time. They had a half pound of "Bubblegum-Kush" to treat themselves to. Montell went to open the door to let Mandy in.

"I tried calling your phone, Montell, but it kept directing me to the voicemail." She said as her and Montell hugged and kissed as she entered.

"Hey, y'all." She spoke to Jamie and Roderick, then passed Montell the food and proceeded to the back room. He accepted the grub from her.

"Aye y'all, this for us." He let his partners know, sat the food on the dining table, and went to the back room to briefly talk with Mandy before they were to get busy working.

Roderick and Jamie got up and went to fix themselves a plate. They then returned, sat back down and continued to talk as they watched the Netflix series they had already been into before Mandy showed up.

"Yo Jamie, that nigga Montell still fuck around with that white chick he met in college all those years ago? That's crazy. I can't believe this shit," Roderick said in good nature.

"Shiddd. Why would he stop? From what I know, the *snow bunny* was the one who held him down throughout the whole bid he served in prison, not to mention the good-ass job she got down at the bank. Tamron was so-so with him."

"Oh, she got a job at the bank, Rod?"

"Hell yeah, nigga! That white bitch got it going on! Montell looking to go legit all the way, and to stay legit. I'm sure she gonna help him out with everything he need to get situated through the bank."

"I bet. But on another tip, what's up with this club thing we been busy trying to put together?" Roderick asked as they continued to talk and Jamie broke it down for him how everything went between he and Felix.

Meanwhile, Montell and Mandy talked in the back room. "I'm sorry about that, Mandy. I had my phone on airplane mode and forgot to turn it off," he said. Thankfully, he lived in a balanced, low crime neighborhood, and Mandy was not put in a vulnerable position.

"It's okay, baby. I understand. I got some good news though."

"And what's that?" he asked.

"I'm up for a promotion from teller to bank manager," she revealed. "There seems to be a few of my coworkers, who feel they're more worthy than me and hate it. But that's fine by me."

"Oh that's good, sweetie. That's wonderful. When will you know?"

"It won't be too much longer. Probably in the next two weeks. It's a strong possibility I'll get it though," she said.

"I'm sure you would. Then you could finally begin buying the home you always say you wanted. One up there on the shores Lake Lanier."

"That's right, baby. I'll finally be able to begin financing a home close to the lake like I always spoke of."

"But anyway, look sweetie. I'mma hit you up later tonight, okay. Me and my homies got a little work to do and some business to discuss," he acknowledged.

"Montell! Please don't tell me you back to your old ways again? Baby, I do not need you getting into any more trouble. No Montell! If it concerns any wrongdoing, please, let it go," Mandy expressed.

"Damn!" he spat and looked on at her in a discerning manner. "Why we got to be up to no good?" He questioned her and wanted to know why she would simply cast such aspersions with no evidence to go on.

"I'm just saying, baby. I don't want this to be a repeat scenario as last time. Look at all the mess you had going on before, and I had no clue you were heavily involved," she reminded and snapped Montell back to reality.

"I understand baby. I get your point. But we ain't got nothing going on fucked up. I'm definitely not trying to go back to prison! Then, I want to be able to get no more of this good *'cunt'* you got me hooked on," he said, changing up his accent to sound like a southern white guy. His sense of humor always made her giggle. He then ran his hand along her thigh until he arrived at her private area.

Chapter 5

Montell gently rubbed between her legs as she sat on the bed with her one leg folded on top the mattress and the other planted on the floor. Mandy had on a thin material pants-suit, and the sensation she felt from Montell's touch, aroused her to action. But he wasn't up for any sex at the moment. He had money and prosperity on his mind, not pussy and busting a nut. They kissed and he escorted her back to the front door and then walked her to her BMW X5.

"Baby, be sure you call me tonight, okay," she insisted.

"I got you, baby. I got you. Now, I'll See you later, okay." he lastly said.

"Okay," she responded, and they pecked the lips of each other then he let her go.

Montell went back inside where his boys were and they got to work. All the while they was at it, Jamie related to Montell all he'd related to Roderick about the meeting he had with the old head, Felix.

"Yeah, Montell, I was mentioning to Rod everything that was said and agreed to between me and my guy who own the titty bar, Felix," Jamie said.

"Oh yeah. I was meaning to ask you about that. What dude talking about?"

Oh, dude all the way with it. He got connections down at city hall and with the mayor bitch. He mentioned something about getting the people down at city hall he tied in with; to increase the amount of alcohol he could sell on his license. Plus, y'all know the nigga a retired Pimp and shit, but still got major love for the game. So, that's a plus for us and an extra stain for him in the life. I figured if it was anything that had to do with girls, getting money, and selling liquor, it would definitely get the nigga's attention. And I be damned! I predicted just right. He say he want in," Jamie let them know.

"So, what all necessary for us to bring to the table?" Montell wanted to know.

"I did tell him it's three of us, and we had fifty thousand apiece."

"And?" Roderick butted in.

"And...he say that's a good start. So, once we hit a lick again with this shit right here," Jamie pointed to the documents and devices they worked on, "we then get busy locating a building to lease, hire an event planner and promotions team, then get out and advertise, calling on nothing but the best and the baddest bitches to come and pop their pussy, shake their asses, and wiggle their titties to get money from all the fellas and a few dyke ho's, who gonna have money to spend up in the spot. It's just as simple as that," Jamie laid it out for them.

"So, what's the plan on *how* we splitting the profit?" Montell inquired.

"Well, due to Felix being the only one with the liquor license, and the necessary connections to get the doors open, he demanded an additional ten percent," Jamie clarified.

"So, in other words, he asking for thirty-five percent?" Montell asked.

"Exactly! And of course, we all get our pay once the workers get paid—bouncers, bartenders, and other personnel. Everybody gotta eat," Jamie related.

"Sounds like a well worked out deal to me," Roderick said once the details were established.

"Myself included," Montell said.

Jamie took another bite of a wing he'd been busy devouring and a sip of soda. "So, everyone is in agreement here?" he asked and gestured with his hand at all three of them in a circular motion.

"I-I captain," said Roderick.

"Yeah, we all on board," said Montell, as he contemplated a way to regain leadership of the group and call shots from behind. He found himself at a disadvantage, being that Jamie was the one to articulate to Felix about the idea of joining partnership on a business venture he came up with the blueprint for. And not only that. Jamie had been free from prison longer than Montell, and had more money than he did, so he assumed Jamie, had no knowledge of the cash and jewelry Montell wisely stashed. No one did

They continued with the business at hand and prepared as much of the claims that day leading into the night as they could, along with the help by video chat of a female friend Jamie had hooked up with, who actually worked at a tax shop. Her name was Adina Simmons. She was a pretty and sexy sweetheart he'd caught. She lived near the Kirkwood section of Atlanta. She knew a lot of street dudes.

***

One Month Later...

Verena hosted her baby shower and the people dear to her were invited. Tiffany wasn't able to make it on a visit prior to. But was there now. She and Chasity. Also, there was Sabrina, the Chief Counselor of the prison who worked for Verena, Tabitha, the Deputy Warden of Care and Treatment at the prison, Mrs. Henrietta Ryan, one of the leading members of the Order of The Eastern Star, a society Verena was a part of. Mrs. Ryan mentored her for years down in Georgia. Of course, Verena's mother, Mrs. Deanne, was present, and so was the aunt, Mrs. Deanne's sibling, Ester. In all, there was about fifteen to twenty women, to celebrate the coming of double new life there with Verena. They had a party of some sort.

When first moving to New Jersey, Verena joined up with the women folk of the Eastern Star and made friends with them. She'd welcomed about six to the baby shower. Three was immigrants into the country: Mrs. Singh, an Indian from New Delhi; Mrs. Soyinka, from Lagos, Nigeria; and Mrs. Heisenberg, from Berlin, Germany. The women provided gifts, and all enjoyed a sensible conversation amongst each other.

Eric was out and about taking care of some business that needed his attention: making contacts with the people of his foreign buddies he'd met while inside, and most definitely, spending time with his Spanish beauty, Joleena. She was of Mexican descent. A member of the narcotics dealing Diaz family.

Her father, uncles, brothers, and cousins, was all into the distribution of Meth and other hard drugs into major cities of the United States. Her family held a stronghold in the northeast portion of the country, in particular, the "Tri-State" area—Pennsylvania, New Jersey, and Delaware. The Diaz family held ties with the Sinaloa Cartel, which was headed by then El Chapo, prior to his arrest. This particular Cartel, controlled parts of the south and the northeast market for Meth and opioids. And the Diaz clan, factored in fairly well in terms of maintaining supply.

Eric and Joleena, met in an awkward type of way. He was fresh to the north out the south and only been in the Garden State two months. They were both out in Atlantic City enjoying the weekend and came into the presence of each other on a couple of occasions at the casinos. Also, at a few of the boxing matches that was going on there. Joleena has two brothers, Robert and Carlos, who are big time into the boxing culture, and so are a lot of her uncles and cousins. They owned a gym and a training center in Trenton, as they promote fights also have boxers contracted.

Two of the fighters out of the Diaz Camp had bouts on the under-cards in AC, and Joleena, her sister Jen, and one of their female cousins, Caitlin wanted to blow some money their fathers provided them, while taking advantage of the night life and relaxing at the AC residency the Diaz family owned there. It was a modest five-bedroom three bath house. This was Eric and Joleena's fourth time meeting up this day, since becoming acquainted.

Eric left home around ten the morning of the baby shower, being he knew such affair, was technically devoted to women, and he didn't want to make it seem as if he was trying to be all stuck up Verena's ass. He drove to Trenton once he had made stops at four properties he owned in Princeton—row houses, which he was having renovated and in the process of being "flipped."

He and Verena owned eight homes in all, along with the floral and garden shop Verena opened for her mother and her aunt to occupy themselves with, and the young assistant they'd hired who knew quite a deal about the business. Her name was Lainey, a white female who was around the same age as Verena. Her experience came from working with her grandparents before they passed away and leaving Lainey, to sell the shop.

Verena and Mrs. Deanne were the purchasers. Part of the deal included Lainey would remain. Mrs. Deanne's sister, Mrs. Ester, was good friends with Lainey's grandmother, Patsy, and it worked out well for Mrs. Ester's sister and her niece, who was looking to continue on with being the owners of the same style of business as they had down in Atlanta.

Eric met up with Joleena, as she wanted to do one of the things thirty-two-year-old females loved to do...go shopping. Eric didn't mind, as he wanted to do the same. The time together would allow them ample opportunity to talk and get to know each other deeper through conversation, and Joleena, could also relate to him the words and the invitations that her brother Robert, the eldest sibling, needed her to convey regarding Eric's inquiry. They hit the highway in Eric's Dodge Durango, en route to New York City, the fashion and media capital of the United States.

"You got any information for me from Rob?" He had asked to initiate the conversation on what he'd asked her to speak with her brother about.

"Yeah. Actually, I do. He told me, he and our father and other brothers, would absolutely be up to personally meeting you at some point in the near future, being I find myself so fond of you in many ways, and you looking to possibly invest your money into the family business."

But Joleena, I wanted to personally speak with Rob myself on a few things he got going on that I want a part of," Eric responded to the information she brought to his attention.

"Sweetheart, I understand all of that. And I specifically worded it to Rob exactly as you asked of me. But it's not how my family operates. And especially not so with a guy I find myself involved with. It simply doesn't work like that. I had to sneak away today so you and I can have this time together. I made the mention of me and my cousin Caitlin, going shopping today. That's how I'd managed to get freedom of space to move about and give you this time."

"And I appreciate it too. Don't ever get the wrong impression that I don't place value and importance on the time we share, because I truly do."

"And I thank you, Eric, for being tolerant and patient with me and the over-protective situations I'm faced with at times."

"Apparently, Joleena, over protection, has a purpose and a meaning to it." Eric reminded, speaking on the power, the status, and the reputation her family held in the world and the line of business that they earned their riches from, the meth and the opioid trade which the Diaz family, tied to the Sinaloa Cartel had murdered, kidnapped, extorted, tortured, and terrorized, to solidify their names, carve out territory, and instill fear in the minds and the hearts of many. The stains of her family came about through brute power and force. Not finesse.

***

Joleena spoke up to what Eric stated, "I'm very conscious of the paranoia my family faces, partly because of whom we are and what we do. But I'm a grown woman, for Christ's Sake. I'm thirty-two now, not twelve or twenty-two," she expressed.

"And you still a female. Very much so vulnerable and not off limits to any other crew that may be aiming to clap back at your family or looking to move the Diaz clan out the way to claim territory. Real talk, Joleena, you being kidnapped for ransom or being hit by a bullet with your father or your brother's name on it, no matter which brother, would give the opposition tremendous leverage to work with and turn your family how they see fit. Never forget that," he stated emphatically.

"I get your point. But enough of all that for right now. My anxieties already get the best of me at times," she said and changed the subject.

By the time they'd gotten through the serious topics of things that which needed to be discussed between them, they was just outside New York City on the highway, and in the process of making an exit to go through the Holland Tunnel. Eric had about $12,000 in cash on him, and a couple of bank debit cards which had a $4,500 weekly limit on each. Joleena had one of her credit cards that possessed $17,000 on it, and her bank card with her to the account the restaurant her family owned in her and Jen's name. This had a $25,000 monthly limit on it. Above all, the two weren't looking to splurge too hard nor waste heavily. They really wanted to share the time together that they were afforded to get to know one another better than they already had.

The beauty about the relationship they were establishing was that no sex had occurred, nor any form of intimacy. Eric wanted to take his time with Joleena and not rush anything as he had with Verena and others prior to. He had a vision and a plan for the two of them, if all was to go well as it showed promise of doing.

Joleena knew nothing at all about Verena. Eric intended to keep it that way, always in the shadows of the other at alternating times, as he split and balanced it between the two.

***

Four Hours Later...

They'd paused briefly for lattes and frappes at a Starbucks in Midtown. Prior to that, their shopping had been at a trade store, and at Versace, Louis Vuitton, and at a Zadig & Voltaire shops along Fifth Avenue. Joleena was a huge fan of the above-named fashion labels. Eric made it his business for them to stop at one of the best Italian tailor shops he'd always read about in the *Robb Report* while in Federal prison.

The name of the place was Loro Piana. He'd gotten sized and measured, then prepaid for two suits to add to his wardrobe. He and Joleena treated one another to gifts as well. Eric bought her a pair of earrings and a diamond friendship ring by David Yurman. A hand purse by Fendi as well. She bought him a watch by Jean Richard, a Titanium Aerospace Black Dial for $4,100. It looked very nice and complemented his skin complexion. Joleena purchased him a couple pair of slacks and button-down shirts by Brooks Brothers. In addition to all she'd bought Eric, she made it a duty to buy her father two of his favorite vices: a bottle of Gran Patron Burdeos, since he loved Tequila, and a box of Cohiba Nicaragua Cigars with a stainless butane lighter.

"I know the gift I bought my father, he's gonna love it," she said with a smile and took a sip of her frappe.

"Any man of your father's stature always take pleasure in something good to drink and something good to smoke. I can't wait to finally meet him. I'm sure we'll take to one another well."

"I'm sure both of you will too. Just give me the time I need to make it happen," she responded to Eric's remark.

"Take all the time you need, baby girl." He said, and they continued to exchange how they felt about each other and on their views of life.

The real truth of Joleena being hesitant about introducing Eric to her father and brothers was, they held racist perceptions about black people, black males in particular. And her father always, since the days she'd been able to remember, encouraged her to date only a man of Mexican descent, "one hundred-percent Mexican," was how he put it to her, and she felt great fear, he wouldn't accept Eric by no means, or even may disown her for as long as she dealt with Eric. The process had to be correct.

Joleena greatly adored Eric, on all levels. He had nice style, specific and exquisite taste, and he made her smile as she never had in none of the previous relationships she'd been involved. Two to be exact.

Their time together in the Big Apple was well spent, and they concluded the trip on a good note. Before departing the city, Eric was sure to reserve them a table—three weeks into the future—at the landmark Seagram Building, the Grill restaurant. He'd seen many advertisements about the eatery and had heard so many wonderful stories here and there on how great the food and the service was. So he felt compelled in a sense to visit. He took the initiative to ensure he and Joleena have the pleasure to do so.

It's ironic in many regards how Eric, had at his home, the more cultivated and formal version of a lady in Verena, the ex-superintendent of a state prison in comparison to the lack thereof in Joleena. And to think, he made the decision to treat the lesser of the two, to a four-star dinner in style and class. Something wasn't adding up.

Was it possible that Eric had grown tired of Verena, and Joleena, was more refreshing to him? Or could it be, Verena, may was pushing Eric away? After all, she'd went so many years without a man in her life. This held a tendency to produce selfish characteristics. And these traits and behavioral issues, she was already very aware of what she had. This wasn't anything new.

It might be safe to say, Verena probably didn't have the graceful wherewithal as a woman, to know how to coexist in a household with a man, being everything happen so fast between her and Eric. But whatever the situation was between her and he, Eric clearly demonstrated, he'd found resolve in the company of Joleena. And he looked to spend more of his time with her in the near future to come.

Chapter 6

The time was just past nine P.M. and Eric returned home to Verena. The majority of the company had left, and the only ones to remain were Tiffany and Chasity. Mrs. Deanne was still up herself, and the women was all talking in the living room when he walked through the door.

"Hi, sweetheart!" Verena greeted, as Eric walked over to where she sat, kissed her, and then took a seat.

He left his shopping bags in his truck, as he didn't want to be put through a series of questions later in the night of his whereabouts.

"Hey babe, Momma Dee, Tiffany, and Chasity," he spoke to everyone.

"We was just discussing the different names you and I had considered to give the babies, and on the future of our kids," Verena said.

"Oh yeah. That's a good thing. I'm glad to see you and your daughter made it to visit us, Tiffany. I've never met your daughter before, but you and I are familiar with one another. Welcome to our home, the both of you," he said to Tiffany and Chasity.

"Well thank you, Eric. It's a pleasure we could be here to provide gifts and welcome life into this world in advance," spoke Chasity.

"Eric and I have so much planned for our babies and our future together," Verena said.

"Well, I hope the two of you got marriage included into the planning. Because the good Lord, don't believe in a man and a woman shacking up, Verena. Especially not so with baby making and motherhood being placed in the mix," Verena's mother Mrs. Deanne injected, while Verena lowered her head and played with her fingertips as her mother spoke.

"We gonna get to that, Momma Dee. I just want to make sure everything right and I'm ready to make that type of life changing transition that being a married man calls for," he responded.

"It seems to me everything already right," Momma Dee nodded her head at Verena to indicate the bulge of her pregnancy, "and you been ready...eight and a half months ago. So, what seems to be the hold up, son?" Momma Dee pressed.

"Well, for one, me and Verena haven't even discussed getting married yet. But we will at some point soon. I'm just not ready for it yet," Eric said and began to stand so he could go to the bedroom and allow the ladies to continue on talking. "Y'all go ahead and talk amongst yourselves. And it was nice to see you again, Tiffany. It was nice to meet you, Chastity," Eric said and walked towards the bedroom.

Eric had been in this same scenario more than enough times throughout Verena's pregnancy. He disliked how his potential mother-in-law would try to pressure him into finally making her daughter his wife.

The fact of the matter was, throughout the private talks between Verena and her mother, Verena would express to Mrs. Deanne how she desperately wants Eric to marry her in due time, and how he should be more than ready at this point in their relationship to make all they had official. But he proved her to be wrong in her assumption each and every time by avoiding the topic all together.

Eric knew Verena put her mother up to saying something to him along the lines of marriage, because he'd get pissed at her and they would go back and forth with words out of frustration until he walked away. Also, he'd told her plain and simple: not to say anything else to him about being married until he brings it up.

Mrs. Deanne felt the time was right, after so long of not being right, while Verena conclude her baby shower of their unborn babies in the presence of the closest people she had in her life: her mother, Tiffany, Chasity, and a large picture of her father on the wall in the living room. But again, Eric wasn't trying to hear any of it, got annoyed, and walked away. He and Verena would talk about it later in the night.

***

Meanwhile...

Nearly four weeks from the day the claims were processed, money began to roll in for Jamie, Montell, and Roderick. They had about fifty of the fraudulent claims they produced returned. The refunds were routed to the debit cards of the names on the list the accounts were created from. The scam crew retrieved the money off the cards and split everything three ways from that point. They was ready to meet up with Felix at the bar so all four of them could discuss the business at hand.

The freed friends who dubbed their crew "3D" now which stood for, "Three Dimensional," made their way to the Westside for the sit down. Upon arriving, Felix met them and escorted the trio to the back of his establishment. Felix had a present with his nephew, along with a silent business partner of his, who he wanted to make part of the business. Everyone shook hands and took a seat.

Felix opened up the conversation, "Greeting fellas! I'm glad y'all could make it, and we all have the opportunity to be owners of a very fine and well-to-do place where gentleman could truly enjoy themselves and spend their money with us," Felix stated.

"And we're glad to be here." Jamie responded, as he became the spokesperson for he and his crew.

"Felix," Jamie continued, "this is my guy Montell here, and Roderick here," he gestured to his right and his left, introducing his partners.

"I got my nephew Geno here, and a long-time business partner of mine here, Dirty Harry. Both I look to bring along with me into this line of business, as we make our rise to the top," Felix informed as he introduced his people.

Chapter 7

Felix's nephew was a known figure in the hood of Bankhead, for formerly being an enforcer for top paying weight dealers who needed muscle and might. He got his start back in the late 1980's and early 1990's working for a big-time holder in the game known on the streets as "Fat Steve." The hood legend and rapper "Shawty Lo," took over Steve's territory when he was arrested and went to the feds. Geno teamed up with him for a time being. Then, BMF invaded the city. The rest is history.

Geno was forty-eight years old now and had been in enough street wars and put in enough work, to take him well into the next life to come.

Through the years, he traded in his stains as an enforcer for that of being a supplier and really began to get to the money in a major way, as he'd gotten down with BMF and elevated to new heights. Then, the Feds came, swept through the A, and completely dismantled the entire Black Mafia regime, from the top to the bottom. Luckily for Geno, he knew how to move, and had avoided those indictments that came down.

Having been missed by the government, Geno counted that as a blessing and stepped away from the game with only a few hundred thousand dollars. He tried going legit. The majority of the money Geno stacked through the years, about five million had gotten invested in a large supply of cocaine that never made it to him. He'd put his money with one of the new leaders of the BMF when Big Meech went down, as they were still supplied 2,000 to 2,500 bricks of cocaine every month.

The work got knocked off and a second round of indictments followed shortly thereafter, leaving Geno and his small crew he led, with their dicks in the dirt. He managed to overcome going completely broke and went into the vehicle detailing business. His uncle tapped him on the proposition that Jamie brought his way, because Geno had the money to put behind Felix, and Geno, was always entertained by the idea of having a hand in the Atlanta club scene. Now was the opportunity to pursue such interest, as his uncle came along at the right time.

Dirty Harry, the silent business partner of Felix, was very similar to his friend in a lot of ways. They were about the same age and had the same background in a sense. He himself, owned a couple of bars, one in the "Bluff," and the other in the Fourth Ward. Dirty Harry also had a used car dealership to generate and keep a steady dollar coming in. On the hood side of things, he was a bookie and ran a sports gambling racket: the "parlay" and "pool" tickets. Nonetheless, it was music to his ears when Felix came to him about what he had in mind through the conversation with Jamie.

"Jamie, I know I didn't mention it to you before. But I've got these two guys here, to back me on every negotiation I become involved in," Felix stated. "This is *my* team here, like you have *your* team there," he added, and waved his hand in gesture to illustrate what he was saying.

"That's not a problem, Felix. It's not a problem at all. I assure you. We've already established how we intend to split the money. You keep thirty-five percent, and we split sixty-five percent," Jamie said.

"Right-Right-Right. But here is the thing. Whose *name* do y'all intend to put down on the lease? Because I don't find it to be such a good idea for y'all putting your own names down on anything," Felix said to express his concern.

"We got all that figured out on our end, Felix," Montell spoke out at that point. "I got my stepfather to be my legal representative." Montell felt the importance to speak up and take charge of the talks, as he still felt he was the rightful leader of their crew and had negotiated way more deals than had Jamie through the previous years.

"Yeah Felix, we got our end handled. Here is a copy of the contract." Jamie pulled out the legal document from a folder. "Read it, take it to your lawyer and have them read over it, then, you sign off on it, get it notarized, and make copies. As you notice, we have already gotten our people to sign and have notarized," Jamie stated.

"I see!" responded Felix.

Jamie put his own name down as he was looking to continue to go legit and have nothing to do with illegal activity from that point moving forward. Montell had his stepfather be his legal hand and Roderick called upon his eldest sister to do so, as she worked for the transit authority in Philly... SEPTA.

"Once we sign everything, the next move will be to establish Escrow accounts and transfer the money," spoke Montell to no objections by Jamie, being he knew Montell was far more business savvy than he.

"I take it as you are more business experienced than my guy Young-blood right there?" inquired Felix.

"I am. He's my guy as well, and he knows my credentials. Our track record is already proven," said Montell to the nodding of heads in agreement by both Jamie and Roderick.

"Y'all know something. Not one time have I heard what the name of the spot gonna be. It's got to have a name and one which will attract as none of the others can do," Felix said.

"Oh, we've already discussed this," Jamie responded.

"Oh yeah! And what's the name?" asked Dirty Harry.

"We decided, we're going to call it...'Club Passion,'" Jamie stated.

"That's deep. That's really deep. But if I must say, it's a bit ordinary. Besides, they got batches of heroin floating around in the city with the same name. They call the shit *'Dog Food Passion.'* So, I would suggest we come up with some extraordinary name to captivate and excite the city with, which it is...a captivating and exciting city," Dirty Harry said.

"And if we had to ask, what would you suggest, Dirty Harry?" Montell asked.

"Well, let me see. The best way for a man or a woman to get the type of attention they truly desire and you know from our experiences Felix is what sells. And being seductive *is* being sexy. So, what I would suggest, is to name the spot 'Club Seduction' or 'Seduction City'," said Dirty Harry.

"I think it's pretty catchy and appealing," Montell said. "Me personally, I like it a lot. I can agree to it. But I'm not by myself on this," he added.

"It does sound fly," entered Roderick. "Besides, every strip club is based on sex appeal and seduction. But I've never heard of any to hold the name 'Seduction.' But 'Seduction City Gentlemen's Night Lounge,' sounds perfect by me. *I* would want to know what a place like that was talking about if I heard a name like it there," Roderick made it known how he felt.

"Well, hey, say no mo'. If that's how y'all feel about the name," Felix spoke up again, "we can go with it. Everybody in agreement?" he asked.

"True," everyone concurred.

Jamie pulled out his pen and wrote in the name 'Seduction City Gentleman's Night Lounge,' on the contract, as opposed to "club." The latter sounded too ratchet for his taste.

"Again, once you get your lawyer to look over it, you sign it, have it notarized, and then, get copies made, we move on to the business of an escrow at that point," Montell reminded.

"Right-right. I got it," responded Felix.

Everyone shook hands and proceeded to move on from the table and back to doing what they were once the meeting ended.

Chapter 8

The relationship issues Verena and Eric faced had gotten worse. This built more by the day. His time out and about from home increased. He didn't give a fatherly presence to the twins like he should have. And he seemed to not give a damn, putting total trust and reliability in Joleena, as their understanding gained strength. This was the ugliest he and Verena's relationship had ever been. He didn't give a shit though. Dude was doing him.

On the other hand Eric and Joleena finally fucked. They now knew what sex was like with each other. It was all that for him. And Joleena now had his nose wide open. This nigga couldn't get enough of what she had to offer. He was in love, but too afraid to admit it, to himself, or to her. This left his feelings for Verena nothing more than a thing of the past. She was a done deal, basically. Why? Because she had let herself go. She was a much older woman than the Spanish heartthrob. She picked up a lot of weight. And she found herself battling with bouts of apathy more often than not. All of this added to the reasons why he was so determined to dump her for someone else, as he had. And now, Eric has forever lost any and all interest he'd once had in her. She was no longer relevant in his eyes. But the younger, more beautiful, and super attractive Joleena was. She'd outshine Verena in every which way imaginable, in Eric's eyes. It was like comparing a flashlight to a star. He felt he made the obvious choice.

To add further insult to injury, the only thing Eric did do whenever he decided to go home, was sleep, or stay up late into the night and play pool to himself, while watching music videos on YouTube in his man-cave.

There were many sleepless nights when Verena would cry to herself until she couldn't no more, or to her mother or either to Tiffany. The only advice they could give her was, she needed to find the strength to someday leave him, or, to do all she could to improve the situation, before she was to lose her goddamn mind and suffer a nervous breakdown. This is how far on the edge she appeared to them.

But other than the issues she went through with Eric, her success in business was coming together. And especially so in the hospitality industry. Specifically, with the investment she'd made with Mrs. Singh. Her Ennisland company now had major contracts in the gambling hub on the east coast of the United States. This being Atlantic City. The casino resorts and hotels brought a lot services to Ennisland and the Singh family, along with other investors in the firm Verena included were looking to capitalize at some point in the future.

At the time when Verena made the initial deposit to become a part of ownership in the company, she got slick about things and approached the situation in a way to help herself and her babies only. Not the baby daddy! What she'd done was, she put on hold the right to add Eric into the fray later down the line, since they hadn't become a married couple as of yet. Every couple that made up the group was married. The Indian business partners of Verena's, valued marriage. It was sacred to them. And it would've been an embarrassment on Verena's part, to be the only one to not have tied the knot.

She was hellbent on talking to Eric again about this. A talk with her mother about the same thing was had. Verena wanted to know the best way to get him to finally propose. Eric didn't give no two fucks no more! His mind was nowhere near focused on being the husband to Verena, let alone, a decent Baby Daddy. However, she went about it anyway, despite knowing she was taking a chance on being cussed the fuck out and ignored even more.

On this one particular night, Eric didn't want to go to bed again and decided to play pool through the wee hours of the night. Verena went down to the basement to at least see him, and to talk maybe. She hadn't laid eyes on dude in just over three days.

Taking a seat in the recliner there, Verena looked at him. She didn't say a word, because she wanted him to speak first and she'd respond. Man, was she in for a big fucking surprise. Eric continued to do what he was doing and made no eye contact whatsoever. Ten minutes passed and still nothing out of him. Verena got teary-eyed and dabbed at them with the night-gown she had on.

Finally, "Eric? Aren't you gonna say something?" she asked.

Still, nothing from him. The tears flowed hard at this point. She began to feel like she was a failure as a woman. As his woman, most notably. But rather she knew it or not, he was so far past the point of being made out as a sucker by her emotions being affected. He was cold-hearted now towards her, in all his wiles and ways.

He paused briefly and propped up on the pool stick. This man just starred at her. She batted her eyes more and shook her head slowly from left to right.

"What is it, Eric? Please tell me, so we can work on fixing things," she spoke out again.

"We!" he retorted with a pinch of sarcasm, leering at her.

Verena's face construed. Her jaw dropped, and she cocked her head to the side while continuing to look at him.

"Yeah, 'we,' were my words. What is it? Would you please tell me, so that 'WE' can fix it, was what I said." She was foolish enough to repeat herself.

"I'm not the one with the problem, Verena."

"Huh! So, I'm the one with the problem now? I'm the one to blame for our problems?" Her emotions kick in more.

"I won't necessarily say it's any 'problems' bu—"

"Well, you did!"

"You see the point I'm making now? Shit just like this could lead to problems. That fucked up attitude and controlling mentality you got, Verena! I done had it with that shit! And then, you keep trying to pressure me to marry yo ass! Got ya momma and ya auntie them, doing the most with you! The fuck! I don't like that shit! At all! I'll get to that point in my own mind and spirit. When I'm ready to! Besides, you and me don't even know what our future look like together anyway!" His words were strong. In a type set they would be **BOLD** faced fonts.

Eric made her realize how he's felt all along.

"So, you ready to leave me now?" She asked the obvious. "Is this what you're leading up to?"

"Ain't nothing here belong to me no way. My name ain't on shit! Not a damn thing! I'm irrelevant to you! And you wonder why I feel the way I feel and think the way I think! The fuck wrong with you!"

"But Eric, here's the thing I don't seem to understand. When and how did this become an issue with you? And after all this time, why you just now saying something about it? About how you feel?"

"It's because... it's a issue. I'm supposed to be the man of the house. And I'm the main reason behind all the money you got. This was before it was an 'us.' Other than the money you already had when we met. And now, you don't seem to love me enough or respect me enough, to see to it, that my name and who I am as a person to you, is recognized. It's like you ashamed of me or something, Verena. Like my past and my criminal history gonna bring disgrace to your name and reputation if it got out we together!"

Dude basically exploded. He reminded Verena in the exchange about what she'd said before to him, that "if and when they do actually marry, she would keep her own name and not take on his. She wanted to remain as Minor. Not become a Mickens."

He continued to vent, "And for some reason, it seems like it's all about the money now with you! What the fuck that be about?"

At this point, Verena kept silent, dropped her head and chin to her breast, and frantically searched around in her mind to think of a speedy comeback to fire in reply. Her words didn't come soon enough before Eric spoke out again.

"Yeah, go ahead and put ya goddamn face in your hands or in your lap! Because just like I thought, it's definitely the truth," he capped.

"No, Eric," she slowly shook her head from left to right. "That's not true. I don't think or feel that way about you, baby."

"Yeah, what the fuck ever! And I'm supposed to believe that shit, right? I'm supposed to just lap it all up and not be as smart as I am and go for that too, I guess?" He felt the need to bring Verena back to the remembrance of the nickname he earned with his high level of IQ and remarkable GPA.

The *Wiz Kid*, she thought. His words "as smart as I am" triggered the memory to back in the days when Montell bragged about how brilliant and knowledgeable Eric was.

"And you actually got the nerve to think I'm gonna marry you and let you have all the power and control in the marriage. Ain't no muthafuckin' way in all hell, will I play myself like that! You got me fucked up!"

"Eric listen, will you? Just hear me out on this, okay? If it ever got out you and me are in a relationship, or married for that matter, I'm more than sure, I could be put under investigation, or even, blackballed from certain things. Let's not forget, I'm an official of the state. You a convicted felon in a Federal court and has been to prison. We don't need that unwarranted attention, baby."

Technically, Verena made a valid point. Or so she thought. Eric didn't agree.

"So, what type of attention would being married bring? I missed that part. I just wanna know from you... miss 'official of the state, as you said?' And since you so concerned about your status and certain things you could be blackballed from, and about your reputation, tell me that much?" he capped.

With that, he laid the pool stick down on the table and began to walk off. He suddenly stopped. "Oh, I almost forgot. You don't wanna take on my name in marriage either, so no attention could be put on us in no type of way, I believe."

"Eric! Don't you walk away from me while we're having this conversation!"

"Man, I'm done talkin', shawty!" he stated and kept it moving, on his way to the front door to get in his car now to leave.

"Eric!" she yells at him. "Eric!" and again. "Don't you walk away from me, dammit!" Verena continued to bark at him as she strutted behind. "I said don't you walk away from me, motherfucker, you!" she said again, then grabbed him by his arm just as he'd opened the front door.

"If you don't get your muthafuckin' hands off me, bitch!" he hissed angrily when he turned. He raised up a hand as if he was about to back-slap her. "With yo fat bad-body ass! Bitch!" His insults were vehement.

"Huh! How dare you talk to me like that, Eric! How dare you, motherfucker!" She responded with a mean mug and flared nostrils.

"Well, I just did! Bitch! Because you need somebody to. And you got the muthafuckin' nerve to be mad and ashamed at me for my past. Hell, you with me! I'm the one who need to be ashamed of yo ass in public, as sorry and as lazy as a woman you ass done got! Goddamn Miss Piggy!!" he insulted again and stepped off, got in his car, and headed towards a diner where he would drink some coffee and eat a slice of pecan pie, his favorite.

Eric left Verena looking and feeling completely stupid. She was dumbfounded about it all. At a total loss for words. He completely caught her off guard with the insults. She just cried more while walking back to the bedroom, then picked up the phone to call Tiffany, to let her know about the argument. She needed more of her advice. Verena had never thought it would come to this between her and Eric. But the thing she didn't keep in mind was, all fairy tales, do come to an end. Sometimes dramatically as their situation seemed to turn out.

Chapter 9

Presently...

At a time after the deal had been sealed about the club business they'd agreed on, Montell and the friend Jamie went cruising throughout the city looking for a building to lease. They were eager to establish. Two weeks passed from the day the meeting with Felix and company happened. The contracts were signed, sealed, and delivered. Together, both camps put together $300,000, and deposited it into an Escrow account. This was put in place for the purpose, and everything was good to go.

A decent spot was located near the Boulevard in the Fourth Ward area of the city. Through the years, this side of ATL had slowly transformed from being a quiet low-key hood to hustle and get money at, to being overtaken by the Crips gang, and the evolution of the *blue flag* being perpetuated for everyone to see. *Thomasville, Four Seasons,* and the entirety of the area, became a haven for the Blue team. But it was a certain level of order and control that came with the territory. It wasn't a *'shoot-em-up bang-bang'* type of environment. The mentality was still a player and to hustle and get money. And since being in this position was in any real nigga's category, it was always and forever with them, to be a player in the game, and stack money.

Montell took charge of the business arrangements with the building they found. He contacted the owner, so to set up a meeting and have a tour of the place. From there, they would have inspectors eventually come and do all that was necessary, so to have the permits granted and the doors could open.

"Yo Jamie, I really feel good about this building here we looking to put our money into, my nigga."

"Shit! Nigga you? Me too!" he responded with a smile and a lot of energy.

"But real talk though, I don't think nothing is gonna make me feel better than I am the moment I get my hands on that nigga Eric and that bitch Verena! I'mma make them muthafuckas' pay! For the old and the new, my nigga!"

"I'm with you on that. But first things first, let's get back the business about the building and opening up the club."

"True dat. You right."

To the surprise of them, the building's owner was able to meet up with them within two hours of being contacted. They were taken for a walk through inside. The place was ideal for all they had in mind. A $10,000 deposit was made then and there through an account transfer from the Escrow, and the process began. "Seduction City" was almost a reality.

***

Up In Philly...

The third standing member of the crew, Roderick, urgently needed to get his ass home. There was very important business for him there and other serious issues he needed to deal with. It had been a shootout in his hood in the "Bad Lands" of north Philly. His family lived near Erie Avenue and German town Avenue. One of the most ruthless spots there. The eldest brother, A-One, along with two others, had been cut down in the vicious streets of Philly by a hail of bullets from an enemy squad.

Aaron Grady, aka "A-One," was the leader of his team. They had a heroin enterprise going in their territory. The cousin of A-One and Roderick, Byron, was one of the casualties of war himself. Byron, aka "Boo-Man," had a promising career in boxing ahead of him, before being killed.

The issue that resulted into the shooting and left three dead, was behind drug territory. It was fought over by soldiers and other dealers on both sides. Also, before the day, a failed hit on the life of Khalib had taken place. He was the leader of the other team. This was ordered by A-One. He went down south to visit while it was supposed to have gone down. It didn't. And as a result, an ambush on A-One was ordered by Khalib. This was completed. A-One was leaving the boxing gym/vehicle detail shop he owned. Boo-Man and A-One's secondary bodyguard—Wendell—got caught in the crossfire.

Roderick was the third oldest of seven kids of their father. A-One made it clear that it will be Roderick, to inherit the majority of his money, if anything ever happened to him. This began the day Roderick graduated high school and A-One putting up the money for him to go to college, some place far away from Philly. Roderick chose Georgia State University to pursue his degree in business.

Roderick was also expected to grab hold of the steering wheel and lead them out in other ways—with both the family *and* the street team. He was to inherit the bank accounts, the businesses, and the residential properties owned by A-One.

As far as available cash was concerned, A-One had hundreds of thousands of dollars, or millions even in narcotics and currency, out in the streets. Possibly more in cash stashed at the houses he owned, or at the houses he shared with the many women he had kids by or fucked on the regular.

Roderick and family needed to hurry and get the money that was stashed away in the safes at all A-One's spots before other shit was to happen and the money would no longer be there. Bitches had the tendency to get grimy.

Upon immediately making it back home, Roderick got together with the family first, then, the second in command to A-One on the streets, his best friend and right-hand Xavier Powell, aka "Big Xav." He was the under-boss of the street family. Through it all, Big Xav was well known by them, and he was a friend of the family. So, he was welcomed to be a part of the conversations that Roderick and family were to have in the days leading up to slain leader's funeral.

They came together to the father's house. "Moses" lived near 33rd and Huntington Ave in north Philly. Roderick was the one who opened and began the talks. "It's good to be back home and to see everybody again. But unfortunately, bro and the fam Boo-Man, no longer with us. And this the reason for us being here, so we can make arranges to have them put at peace eternally."

"Yo bro, them bitch-ass niggaz gotta pay for the shit they done! Like for real, they do! And I'm ready to get busy, my nigga!" said the fiery sister of theirs. Lea was a bit of a live-wire herself. She loved to date bold dangerous dudes. Compatible attitudes basically.

"Calm down, Lea, calm down. I plan to address all this and more. But what I'm trying to figure out is, who's the one person responsible? Who gave the order? Anybody know?" Roderick had asked.

Royce Grady, the fourth born son, wanted to answer. "Well, the streets saying, it was the nigga Khalib from down by the old Richard Allen area on Giraud Ave. He put his boys up to doing it. Word is, they was looking to expand some type of way, and Khalib and bro got into a dispute about things a while back. They had a war of words of some sort at a bar, and shit snowballed from there," he related.

"Xav, you familiar with any of this?" Rod asked.

"Yeah. A-One and dude did get into it. This was during the time when A-One went down to Atlanta for those weeks to spend time with you there. Remember? And we had the squad on top of shit, but we couldn't never locate the nigga to put an end to what he was talking about. But that's neither here nor there now. The squad *definitely* in the process of seeing to it that the ops feel the wrath of their error!" Xav let everyone know. He concluded with anything else on the subject.

"Rod, you already know A-One wanted me to see to it that you be the one to take over for him, right?" the father spoke up and said.

"Yeah pops. Everybody here already know this," Roderick said.

"Okay. Understood. But I'm in pain, y'all. I am. Because shouldn't no parent have to ever go through the pain and the grief associated with losing a child. Shouldn't no parent have to go through this," stated Mr. Ervin Grady, the man affectionately known by his nickname of 'Moses.' He really took the death of his eldest son to heart. The old man wept nonstop since the moment of getting the news.

Roderick stood to his feet and walked over to console their dad. "Everything gonna be all right, pops. Everything's gonna be all right. An eye for an eye, and a tooth for a tooth, is what the good book says, right?"

The father looked up into the eyes of Roderick and declared, "you damn right it does! And y'all gotta be sure to get their's!"

Roderick and crew had more problems on their hands than they knew, going up against the nigga Khalib and his team. He was the cousin to a street psycho named, Kaboni Savage, a nigga that probably had more bodies under his belt than he had people that liked him. His family included. There was definitely a tough showdown looming.

Chapter 10

Weeks Later...

Eric and Verena finished with last preparations they had to make and made the necessary choices they felt relevant to bring the twins into this world. Also, they settled on the names Eric II and Erica. The baby-shower was wonderful; their living situation and financial status were in a good space; and the progress made by them in a different state was providing to be about something. This could potentially put them on pace to becoming a part of the status-quo there in New Jersey, as Verena wouldn't have it no other way, since she was the type of high-class lady she'd worked so hard at positioning herself to be.

However, there was two problems that Verena was forced to battle with in her relationship with Eric: One; he hadn't even so much as uttered the words "getting married" out of his mouth; and two, his time away from home go worse. He wasn't spending it there with her.

What he'd began with Joleena, got good and they were headed in the direction Eric always wanted them to go in. He was finally invited to her dads to have dinner with them and talk over a few things. Eric needed to introduce himself to them. Joleena's brothers, her sister, and her female cousin she's close to, were to also be there. The mother passed away three years ago from breast cancer.

While at the house enjoying a well-prepared Mexican dish coincidentally and drinking on the best wine they had to offer, Eric, was bombarded with a shit load of questions by a bunch of people he felt pressured to answer up to. This was if he wanted the prize in Joleena he was working so hard to have. Some of her family members were speaking in English and the rest in Spanish. Eric only understands the language he spoke. He felt good about the process. And Joleena did give a heads up to him that her family would put him through this. But he was okay with it, because he wanted the prize at the end of the rainbow. And having Joleena, and being in direct contact with the Diaz clan and the drugs they supplied, along with the boxing enterprise and sports business he could get behind his two cousins with that boxed, all added up to success for him in these ways.

When the dinner was over, the *real* business began. Joleena's father, her brothers, and Eric, all moved to the back room of the house to talk more.

Pappa Diaz began. "From what I was told, Eric," began Oscar, "you have done a little time in the past. Is this so?"

"Something like that. Me and my guys were into the white-collar thing for a while."

"The financial thing, huh?" the brother Robert chimed in to say.

"Yeah, that."

"Joleena told me *everything* about the two of you," spoke Poppa Diaz again.

"*Everything?* "

"Yes, *everything*. She wants my blessings."

"I understand. A father does need to give permission to a guy his daughter wants to date."

Poppa Diaz said, "What is interesting to me, is the fact that my daughter is really fond of you. She tells me you are very genuine and sincere. How charming and respectful you are of her and her body. Joleena says you haven't so much as pressed her once about sex." He seemed to be impressed.

Eric utilized the opportunity to put on his charm so to flatter Poppa Diaz. *"No-she-didn't,* did she?" he said, now smiling heavily. "Did Joleena tell you all our business?

Because as shy as she is, I wouldn't have thought that." he made known. The man he was face-to-face with, was the one he wanted to give him the go-ahead to continue dating his daughter.

"I see you two really getting acquainted with each another, for you to know about her shy personality."

Eric mentioned. "We talk a lot in person and on the phone."

"But here is the thing I *really* wanna know from you, because Joleena didn't seem to specify *exactly* what your status was with any another woman. Are you a married man?" Poppa Diaz asked bluntly.

"No! I'm not, Señor," dude responded, and held out his hand to demonstrate he had no ring.

"That's a good start for you. I'm also made known that you are business savvy and stable with money." The father turned the discussion to lean towards business and prioritizing.

"I'm straight in the right way."

"What makes you so interested in wanting to become a part of the business me and my family have going?" the father wanted to know.

Eric knew Poppa Diaz was strictly referring to the dope they dealt in. He had to think long and deep before replying. He finally did.

"My interests in the business you and your family got, could make me a rich man and expand the empire *I'm* looking to personally build for me and mine. With my own hands. One brick and one scam on the government at a time. And at the same time, I know it'll make you happy, Señor, to know your daughter is involved with someone who's serious about money and being stable and committed to doing the work hand-in-hand with her family. Led by you, of course I also own property too, and wanna have a hand in the boxing world with Robert," Eric added while looking back and forth from Poppa Diaz to Robert, to see their reactions behind his words.

"I think we could get to like this guy, Poppa," Carlos said, speaking up for the first time.

"I believe we could too," said Sandro, the other brother present.

"It seems my boys here, likes the choice in a man their sister has made, Eric."

"I was definitely hoping so," he replied to the compliment with a smile.

They all enjoyed a good laugh together and began to kick shit. Before the night ended at the Diaz family house, Poppa Diaz let Eric know he was okay with him dealing with his daughter, and he would consider the proposition of having him supplied with their dope at some point in the future. Eric was told that he may wanted to get busy building a distro network of his own to help get rid of the supply, if it was decided to let him in on the business.

Robert got into it with him in discussion on the sport of boxing and wanted to know, *"did he have any fighters on hand who could become a part of the boxing team?"* he had asked.

Eric had two cousins down in Georgia he wanted to move to the north with him and get them into professional fighting. This could be an additional avenue he could pour money into from the sell of the products he would eventually be supplied by Poppa Diaz.

Everything with the relationship between Eric and Joleena was going well, and the quality time they shared, would increase over the next months to come. But Verena, on the other hand would have a lot to say about Eric being out from home so much, as he was beginning to demonstrate he was capable of doing. Her infuriating attitude is to take a heavy toll on their relationship. Things had the potential to go crazy.

Chapter 11

The doors to "Seduction City Gentleman's Night Lounge," finally opened to the city of Atlanta and all surroundings. A party promoter and event group were hired by Seduction City Investment Group—basically Montell, Jamie, Roderick, Felix, and Dirty Harry. They'd been in business about six days now and had nothing but some of the best and most talented dancers performing each night. Their days of business were Thursdays, Fridays, and Saturdays. Montell proved to be the smarter of them all, as it related to the girls. He began a management group under Tamron's name and offered the girls contracts that wanted to make money from videos, advertisements, and other media related ventures.

Felix and Dirty Harry made it a business to show their faces at times, but most often, the two old heads preferred to stay behind the scenes and in the comfort of the bars they owned across town. But Felix made sure to have Geno maintain a thorough presence at the spot and represent their side of the ownership. Geno held plans himself, to lay his own infrastructure within the interior of Seduction City. He was hellbent on utilizing the power he still had from people who knew him from his days of glory in the ranks of BMF.

Montell had plans of his own too. Tamron and many others, had put the idea in his head to look into or possibly going ahead and invest in the popular club drugs of the day: *Molly, Ecstasy, Xans, Percs, Flaka,* etc. The way it was put to him was, "he couldn't go wrong by catering to the crowd that partied there at their club. He could have it both ways, business and pleasure.

Montell figured he could make anywhere from $10,000 to $20,000 or more on the side with his product over a two-to-three-day time frame without any of the others knowing a thing. Indeed, drugs was not his signature hustle, and they had a crew policy, no one would get into that line of business because the way things fell apart with Rico and the 'Jimmy Smack' situation. But Montell, on his own accord, felt it was time to move on from income tax scams and other white-collar thievery, and get into the world of building a street team and transforming himself into a bona fide boss in the underworld, much like the many thoroughbreds he grew up around and looked up to in Albany and in Atlanta. A guy named Junior Pete in Albany, and Puerto Rican Johnny in Atlanta.

While in the Feds, he met legendary hood stars and soaked up the street wisdom they had to offer. He maintained in his mind about someone being a feared and respected nigga in the underworld, that it would give them a chance to rise to power, call shots, and issue orders to the people. At least to the ones that were intent on being loyal and committed to the team he would build from scratch. He figured if he was already that type of nigga, neither the bitch Verena, Eric, *their babies,* or that fuck-nigga Rico, would still be alive to laugh at how they took from him, snitched on him, or disrespected him, in the way they all had, so thought Montell.

He'd been had all of them put to death a long time ago! But their date with the grim reaper would come at some point or another. All needed was to leave them space to come out of hiding, then, he could get them.

But on the flip side of things, Montell accepted the suggestion of the difficult girlfriend, Tamron, and made the decision to put up a $100,000 into Meth, Molly, Ecstasy, Percs, and Flakka. The 'Fab Five' Montell dubbed the product he wanted to deal in. He was serious about having a thriving enterprise of his own. He felt it had come time to distance himself from Jamie and Roderick outside of the club.

They each were budding entities in their own rights and needed to separate so as to grow and prosper how they saw fit for themselves. This was much in line like Jay-Z, Dame Dash, Kareem Biggs, and the Rocafella family break up.

Montell was at Tamron's house chilling. They were spending quality time this weekend when the conversation went to the business. "Say T-Baby, I thought over everything you and me talked about with getting into *that* life," he said.

"Is that right? I figured you'd began to see it my way before long," she responded to his words as they lay on the bed watching the TV series *The Handmaid's Tale* on Hulu.

Tamron had a house in Dekalb, Georgia her parents left her. The mother passed away from the flu when Tamron was only nine, and her father, was a police officer with the city of Atlanta, that was killed in the line of duty during a jewelry store robbery when Tamron was fifteen. She's thirty now and was raised by her father's brother and his wife. They had a daughter who was the same age as Tamron. They're still close to this very day. Landy Bryce is her name.

"So, what made you consider?" she asked.

"The main thing was, I began to feel like me and my niggaz been around each other too long and knew one another's business too fuckin' much. And not only that. I had also got arrested, convicted, and went to prison, because a nigga I thought was my friend, fucked me over! Who's to say it won't happen again?" He was emphatic in his tone of voice.

Tamron raised up on her elbow while facing Montell, looked him square in the eyes, then expressed exactly what she was thinking. "Now see, Montell. See. That's the *you* I'm so afraid to be involved with. The *grown man* you. The mature and ready to do his thing in the business world, you.

This version, I'm scared I might lose, behind the same reasons you just said you wanna separate yourself from your boys, Jamie and Rod, for. Because y'all been around each other too long and know each other's business too well. I shouldn't have never said anything to you on that. I put my foot in my mouth then, I now know.

"Well, next time, you know to be careful with what you ask for," he said and then chuckled.

"So, I guess now I got to worry about losing you, huh?"

"Have you lost me yet? How long we been fuckin' around? It's been a long ride, right? Through my prison bid and all too, right?"

"Yeah, through it all."

"So, why would I wanna just up and let a solid girl like you go, all because I'm looking to get prioritized and more business minded than I have been in my life? If anything, I'm gonna bring you with me. Besides, it's *you* who's responsible for helping me grow into my own. So, why not have you by my side to experience success with once I make it through the ranks?"

"You make very good points, Montell. I just don't wanna lose you, to no one else or to the system again, okay," she said, then they kissed.

"Now, here is the plan I've got in mind. I wanna deal in the new age stuff—Meth, Molly, E, Percs, and Flakka. I nicknamed these muthafuckas' the 'Fab Five,' if you must know," he said while smiling.

"You what?" Tamron blurted while on the verge of laughing at Montell.

"I nicknamed the work I wanted to get into, the 'Fab Five,' That's our code word now, okay."

"I'm with it, baby, I'm with it. I just wanna see us rise above and get to the money together. Because at all cost we gotta secure the bag *together*, Montell. As a couple, my nigga. I'm not complete without you. I wanna stay right here by your side through it all."

"Don't worry, Tamron. We good. We good, baby. I just need to get busy trying to find a plug to supply me. I got somebody in mind that I linked up with in the feds. A Spanish cat. And he told me to be *sure* to get in touch when I got out. He got forty years to do, but his brothers and family, big time. It could be an option of mine to explore."

"Well, I got two things going in my favor to help us make our way to the top too. Actually, I got *three* things in my favor," she said.

"And what's those?"

"For one, my uncle, as you may remember, is a high ranked detective with the Atlanta Police Department. Two; I've got a degree in Spanish. And three; I got a muthafuckin' passport to travel with, my nigga."

"Damn! I forgot you still have your passport, T-Baby."

"You bet, I do. All those goddamn cruises and vacations to the D.R., Jamaica, Cancun, and those other places you and me used to go. I really enjoyed those times, Montell."

"I know you did. But unfortunately, for me, I lost my passport rights when I got convicted. My right to have guns, and all types of other rights I once had. But it ain't no sweat though. I still got the most powerful piece on the chessboard by the side of the King, and that's my queen, you," he said with a smile as he and Tamron began to kiss again.

"That's right baby, you got me, your queen," she responded and smiled herself. The two continued to talk and make plans on how they were to approach the future business and deals on party drugs they were eager to sell. The planning would manifest sooner rather than later.

Chapter 12

In The Meantime...

As Mandy was performing her duties at work in the bank, attending her teller space, in walked someone she absolutely did not want to see, let alone, be bothered with. It was her ex-boyfriend, Dylan. He'd not long relapsed and went back to being a dope-head on Meth and other Opioids he loved to put into his body. His clothes were dirty and scraggly, and he had a terrible odor about himself, as he hadn't showered in probably twenty days, nor had any sleep. He'd been up rolling nonstop—from dusk to dawn—and had no plans to pipe down any time soon. He needed money. Dude wanted to get high more and Mandy was his only option, his last resort. Or he could go out and stick up a gas station, a grocery store, or something else for an amount of cash he wanted. At all cost something had to give.

Mandy had two customers in line. She happened to look up and saw the unwanted visitor. His head roved from left to right, then right to left, in search for her. She was finally spotted. Dude then staggered in the direction where she stood.

"Mandy!" he called out for her. "I need to talk to you, please." This fool hopped in line to await his opportunity to get closer. He fidgeted and moved uncontrollably, as he dug his hands down in his dirty jean pants pockets, fishing for nothing.

"Mandy! Didn't you hear me? I said, I need to talk to you!" His words got louder.

"I'm working, Dylan. What do you want?" she stated. "Excuse me ma'am. I apologize for this." An apology was offered to the customer in the line in front of Dylan. The lady turned to get a look at who it was Mandy was talking to. She was appalled at his appearance and smell.

Dylan spoke up again, "I said, I need to talk to you. I'm in need of money. I wanna, uh, to get high some more and I need you to give me some money to do it with. You know I still love you, don't you, Mandy," he spat.

Mandy continued to ignore him, as she was totally embarrassed beyond all her imagination she'd be. She never looked up at Dylan to give him any eye contact. Just continued to be of good service to the elder lady she attended to.

Once the old lady moved on from Mandy and about her way out the door, there was no one in between the two from that point. She attempted to play the professional role on Dylan. "Hello sir! Welcome to first Citizens National Bank. How may I help you?" she stated.

"Are you being serious right now, Mandy?" he responded.

She had to hurry and place both hands over her mouth and nose to keep from throwing up, due to how foul his breath was. It smelled as if he'd eaten a hot bowl of maggots and washed it down with a big gulp of three-week-old dumpster juice.

"Dylan, I don't care to talk to you at all, let along, give you any money. I despise your very presence, and I totally regret I ever had anything to do with you! So, what do you want now?" she spat.

"You fucking bitch, you! How dare you talk to me like that!" he responded and pointed his finger in her face, causing her to step back, capturing the attention of her supervisor, the bank manager.

He walked over to assess the situation.

"Miss Barfield, is everything okay over here?" he asked of Mandy.

"Yes sir, Mr. Mimms. Everything here is fine. It's just my ex-boyfriend, briefly stopping by to say hi, and is now leaving. Aren't you, Dylan," she said and tried to urge him to go.

"Yeah, sir, I was stopping by to say hello, and to also get my girlfriend here, to give me a few dollars to have some fun with. Pardon my French, but I'm trying to go get *fucked up,*" he said to the supervisor and smiled, exposing those rotting teeth of his the dope use caused.

"Sir, we don't use inappropriate language in this place of business," said Mr. Mimms, "and if you're done, I'd like to ask you to be going on about your way," he added while standing close to Mandy and waiting on the next move of Dylan.

"You uppity bastard, you! Didn't you just hear me? I said, Mandy there," he pointed at her, "is my girlfriend. And I stopped by to get her to give me some money. What part of that that shit was not clear?"

"I ain't got nothing for you. So go!"

Dylan gave her one of those cold stares as he had before to let her know he was serious as a heart attack. He'd also slapped her a time or two in the past, in the aftermath of these same style of grimaces.

"I'm not going nowhere, until you give me what I came here to see you for," he declared.

Mr. Mimms intervened again, "sir, if you're not looking to do any business, then I'm going to have to ask you to leave the premises. Or, I'll be forced to call the police," he warned.

"So, leave, Dylan. And never come back here again."

"You fucking bitch! Come here!" he cussed her, then lunged forward and grabbed the poor girl by her shirt.

"Stop Dylan! No! Stop!" she said and frantically tried to break free from his clutch. She couldn't.

Mr. Mimms began to beat Dylan on the arm with his fist in defense of Mandy. Dylan slapped her twice then turned and began to fight with the supervisor.

"Someone call the police, now!" Mr. Mimms instructed, as one of the other female employees pulled out a small container of mace, then sprayed Dylan in the eyes. He began to scream to the top of his lungs behind the burning effect, while at the same time, trying to wipe his face with his right hand and yanking on Mandy with his left. Two other male employees came to assist. They finally subdued Dylan and had him pinned to the floor.

Ten minutes later, the Atlanta PD arrived to arrest this lunatic for assault, disorderly conduct, resisting arrest, and public intoxication. His arrest triggered a violation of his probation, and a possession of narcotics charge, being the probation officer ordered Dylan's blood be drawn and tested. He was positive for meth.

It was a very embarrassing day for Mandy, and especially so, being she had went up for promotion to be the bank manager and to have an increase in her income. The incident didn't have any negative effects on what she was trying to do at her place of employment. Mandy was still best suited for the job. No doubt.

Chapter 13

Montell stood on business and finally get in touch with the brother of the guy he'd met in prison and became friends with. The fellow inmate of Montell at the time, a Raul Mendoza, is of Colombia descent. His family were prominent figures in one of the most powerful cartels out of Colombia. Raul's brother—Petey—was already informed by Raul, that Montell would eventually be contacting him to set up a line of business. He figured he'd find success in enticing Montell to get involved with dope dealing. And when Montell initiate the call, Petey was ready to negotiate.

Pete's English was not all too good, as he'd only visited America on a few occasions. This was the area Tamron would play a crucial role, with her being learned in the Spanish language. She would make it her business to know all of the business between Montell and his Colombian connections. She would become Montell's most trusted translator.

Tamron could relate to Pete all she saw fit and vice versa, in regard to Montell. And at the same time, she had a passport, and would more than likely be called on to travel to Bogota to arrange deals for her man with his plug. The first conversation was a success.

"Yes, Montell—'*Mo,*'" said Pete. "My brother tells me that you are a very brilliant guy."

"I can be when I choose too."

"You uh, you are aware, uh, on my English here is, not all too good, right?" Pete makes it clear to Montell of his unlearned abilities in his limited knowing of the English language.

"I know, Pete. Raul told me about his family. And yes, I do have a remedy for this."

"Huh?" Pete didn't quite understand him.

"I said, I've got a remedy for this. I have my girlfriend here with me—my Señorita—she knows Spanish."

"Oh yeah, many Señoritas here, Mo," Pete mistakenly thought he'd said.

Montell shook his head and smiled. Thankfully, he did have Tamron there by his side to properly translate for him. He put her on speaker phone.

She clearly related in Pete's native language who she was and everything Montell needed her to convey. Pete, was impressed, and told Montell, from there on out, he wanted Tamron, to translate for him, so it wouldn't be any misunderstandings on what was said. Montell agreed, then they got into the discussion on the business at hand a $100,000 he wanted to spend on a combination of different drugs: his 'Fab Five.'

Pete already had people in the states that distributed his products to the customers who was to be supplied. Atlanta was one of their main distribution hubs for the cartel Pete and their family worked for. He would have someone verbally coach Montell on how to establish accounts which was to be tied into the businesses he and his people owned in the states. They had coffee houses and South American Spice Shops where food seasoning and herbs were sold. The majority of the money from drug deals Pete's people made was wired through bank transfers and legitimate business accounts. The Cartel had a sophisticated format on how they'd manipulated the financial infrastructures to suit them and what they had going on, so as to not have their money confiscated by the government, and this way made the drug trade far better for them in avoiding potential investigations and prosecutions.

Montell was definitely familiar with business and finances. Also, he had Mandy on the side to handle the transactions at the bank for him. There were shell corporations he had in mind to eventually establish for this, once business gets to booming.

The blueprint to his operation was laid out, and Tamron knew everything about everything there was to know, a reality Montell was not too excited about, but had to go along with, due to how involved she'd became at the very beginning.

The crazy part about it was, Tamron, now knew how important her role was to Montell and Pete. And if Montell had ever gotten wrong or out of line with her, she could turn him like a thumbscrew to make him act right, and make herself an indispensable figure in the world of Montell she now play a major part in. Tamron would be able to really transform herself into the "boss-bitch of the city," she swore by God she'd someday become, at the point of Montell sending her to Colombia, to meet Pete and be the voice of him at Pete's negotiation table. There was a lot to come, and Tamron, was oh so ready to get busy with it. So was Montell.

Chapter 14

The twins Eric Jr and Erica, were both healthy as ever and growing fast. They were almost two months in age and required plenty of attention from mommy and daddy. Verena found herself doing everything and began to get really frustrated and angry at the fact Eric offered only little help, and stayed gone from home more than anything.

One night, he came in the house early. Verena had a lot on her mind she wanted to get off and dig down to the bottom of. She wanted all the issues faced with him discussed. They were both sitting on the bed watching *Animal kingdom* on TV. Verena went in on him then and there with her words.

"Eric, I got a few things I wanna ask you. A few things I wanna talk about too. Okay," she'd began.

"Okay. What's good, sweetie?"

"Is it somebody else?" she flat out asked.

"No! Why you ask?" he lied, then wanted to know her reason for this particular question.

"Because it's obvious to me, Eric. That's why I asked."

"Well, no it's not. And if it was, I'd just tell you. I wouldn't even waste anymore of your time, let alone my own."

"Eric..." she said again, then became emotional. She began to cry from the thought of how fucked up her relationship with him had become. "Eric look. What we have was supposed to never have been this one-sided. I'm here all day every day with our babies—"

"And I'm out handling business, *all day every day,* to make sure that the future is gonna be right for us and our babies," he cut her off to say.

The tears flowed as she built up the will to fully express to him exactly how she felt. To maybe bring an end to the loneliness she experienced as well, although she was in a relationship with him.

"But Eric, you got to understand my point of view here. You give me no attention. We don't go out together anymore. You're barely home. What else am I to believe?" She wanted to know his answer to her questions. "You don't even do your best to at least make me feel like I'm your woman anymore. How did everything fall apart so fast in one year? In only one year, Eric. That's what I wanna know?"

"Well, what do you want me to do from here on out, Verena? Huh? What do you want?" He turned the line of questions on her.

"I want for you to get back to being the dude I fell in love with. I want you to bring yourself back to mind on everything we had made plans to do. For us to be a power couple and enter the business world of our liking, then, rise above. And over all, Eric, I want you to stop making me feel unwanted. Stop making me feel unappreciated. And stop making me feel like I'm a nobody to you. Okay." She held back no more.

"That's on you if you feel the way you do. It's not behind something I'm doing wrong," he responded cold bloodily.

"Eric. This is not the life I had in mind for myself when I made the decision to stop being a warden to be with you. This is *not* the life I had in mind, damn it!" she emphatically stated. "I gave in to you. I believed in you. And I trusted you. I feel betrayed. You *crossed* me, nigga!"

"Well, this damn sure wasn't the life *I* had in mind for myself either! The fuck you mean! But here I am, right. Here I am. Way in another state from home and family, trying to adjust to living a life I'm not familiar with, but willing to give it a try. *Your* choice of lifestyle, that is to say. And I got kids by a woman I'm in a relationship with that's also been involved with one of my best friends before me!"

"Oh, okay! I see where we going with this here, again! *Now* I see. We back on the subject of me and Montell again, ain't we?" she said, as she sat up straight, her hands on her hips, and mouth wide while eyeing Eric in disbelief at his words.

"Verena, that's gonna always be a issue between us. I struggle in dealing with it damn near every day."

"Eric, you made a choice to be with me. You the one who got me pregnant. You the one that agreed to move here with me and my momma. Now, it's all going on, you got something to say about it. Why?" she asked, her head hanging low.

"It's just some bullshit for me personally, to know I went against the code, to be with you. But again, that's neither here nor there at this point," he said in a frank manner.

"Well, why do you continue to make it a continuing issue, since we a year past it now?"

"I don't know, Verena. I really don't know. But we'll get it right and be the success we supposed to be. Come here sweetie," he said, then pulled Verena close to him and they began to kiss romantically.

Eric had to cut back on the negative energy he dished out to Verena. He was at the point of realizing how beneficial she was to him. From a business perspective. Because of her credentials and solidification as a state official.

Truth be told, Verena had a lot of power with her knowledge of administration and could always tap into it when she so chose to. This was taken from the position she once had. And by potentially getting another job working for the state of New Jersey, in addition to being a businesswoman, she'd be empowered again, and have an opportunity to be in total control.

Eric needed her to remain a happy lady with him, so he would be able to carry out the plans and agenda he had designs to do. This was of course in the world of business that he wanted to play. Their relationship couldn't suffer any damage by no means. Especially not so because he made the decision to date a younger female and get access to her family, who in essence, was a connection to the product he wanted to be involved with and get money fast. He had to be smooth with how he now moved. And then, he could get out the game a paid man and continue on a legit path towards the land of milk and honey—in a prosperous and thriving career as a completely legit businessman—within a millionaire's tax bracket.

Verena spoke out more in the conversation they were having, because there was something she really wanted to relate to him, from a business standpoint.

"Since you always seem to be on the subject of business, how about, my Indian friend, Nerandra Singh, offered me the opportunity to invest into her and her husband's hospitality group, Ennisland," she informed.

"Really? That's great sweetie. That is really great," Eric responded.

"Yeah. You know they own a slew of hotels and other establishments here in New Jersey and in New York. Ennisland is a offshoot to the parent company that was created and developed by a body of rich and powerful Indian immigrants that came here and began to buy up everything. And especially in the hospitality industry they're firmly planted at."

"How did you two even get on the subject?" He was curious to know. From his knowledge and experience of dealing with these kind of Indians in Georgia, if they let somebody from outside their race into business with them, it had to be something real serious that the outsider had to offer. Especially so for a "black woman," in exchange for them to have the Indians let them put their money with theirs, and eventually profit in the way that they do.

Little did Eric know, these kind of Indians in the north, were totally different in mentality than those in the south.

"Well, actually, Nerandra and I are part of the same sorority order. And it's a mandatory duty of ours to come together in business and gain strength. *Together*, that is. At any opportunity we get. We are encouraged to do so. It's a powerful sisterhood we have, Eric. That's how we got onto the subject," she made mention of.

"Oh, okay. Y'all gotta boss up. I forgot about that society shit you're a member of. But I know how it works too. She has an available space for you in her business, but what you gonna offer in addition to money?"

"Eric, I'm a sworn official of a state that so happen to have transferred all of my credentials to *this* state. I got political power and influence that could help her get permits from the state, or any other governing body she may need to ever go to, for that matter. The group is looking to make a splash in Trenton and Cherry Hill, New Jersey. That's in the next six months or so," she related.

"Well stated. Much understood sweetie."

"And this could be a move to really put us in the loop and set us up for the type of success we always wanted and long prepared ourselves for, baby."

"How much money upfront is Miss Singh asking for?"

"I was told to have a million dollars in five installments. This will give us roughly a four to five percent stake in ownership to the group. Roughly a hundred dollars of every one thousand."

"That's not bad at all, sweetie. It ain't. How soon do you need to transfer the money to them?"

"We've got time. We do have that. I only need to let her know we want in. And they require us to put down a fifty-thousand-dollar deposit and then they'll began taking care of the paperwork."

"Okay, go ahead and make it happen. I definitely want us to get in on it. Yeah. Absolutely."

Their talking continued down the line of the investment they were soon to make. Eric became excited at how good life had begun to turn out for him after prison and in another state, opposite the minor problems he went through with Verena. He was evolving into a boss in his own right. Now all was left, was for him to get out and build a team. He was going to need a squad to move the product Joleena's father and brother was going to start him out with. He was a star on the rise.

Chapter 15

The Next State Over...

In Pennsylvania, Roderick was eager to get back at home to Philly from Atlanta. He now read and had all that was necessary to carry out the wishes of his murdered brother, A-One. The order given to Big Xav, BK, and the rest of the crew, to 'smash on site,' the nigga Khalib, or, any family member of his, if they were to ever cross paths. Xav knew Khalib and his people better than Roderick did, and felt it was only a matter of time before bullets would begin to fly and someone on their side—team Khalib—be put down and out.

The sun was barely set, as Big Xav, along with one of the young soldiers on the team, Yammi, were out cruising through the streets of the north, when they spotted a car. It was one they knew who the owner of it belonged to. It was a smoke gray colored Mercedes Benz S-Class 600 series, one of the luxury vehicles the dude Khalib owned. They were headed north on Broad Street near Glenwood Ave, close to Joe Frazier's former gym. The driver of the Benz and the passenger with them, was headed in the opposite direction going south towards Center City, possibly to the Girard Ave area, Khalib's neck of the woods.

"Yo! How 'bout I know who car that is right there?" Xav said to his young gunner, Yammi, and immediately began to turn around and follow in the direction of the Benz. He was in one of his low key rides, a Chevy Malibu, a new model joint. He bent two blocks then got back on Broad and spotted the Benz once more.

Yammi picked up on the adrenaline and the elevation of eagerness in Big Xav's demeanor. It indicated they may was about to see some action.

"Yo Yam'! You got yo hammer on you, right?"

"Hell yeah, bro! Da hell is wrong with you, asking me something like that, nigga!" the young assassin responded and then pulled his Nine Millimeter from his waistline and cocked it, putting one in the chamber.

"That's that nigga Khalib's car, Yam!"

"Oh word! That bitch-ass nigga gotta pay for the lick he put on A-One and them!"

"Muthafuckin' right, he do!"

The Benz stopped at the red light of Broad and Lehigh Avenue. Xav was three cars behind. The light turned green and the Benz glided through the intersection, then slowed while easing to the middle lane looking to go left into the self service car wash. Xav passed by to stealthy to know exactly what was the intended destination the driver of the Benz was looking to go. He banged a right two blocks down, then another right, and another onto Lehigh Ave, heading back towards Broad Street. Xav pulled into the *Sunoco* gas station on the corner and posted up at an angle of where he was facing the direction of the car wash. He and Yammi saw two guys get out the Benz. Neither one was the main target, Khalib. However, those in the car, they were valuable pieces in Khalib's circle, that could play a part in the grand scheme of things, a possible "King's Ransom," so to speak.

Khalib was the only nigga in the city, who owned a 600 Benz—smoke gray in color—that had a chrome plate on the front that read '4X LIFESTYLE' (hence: Big Boy Lifestyle), as he was a fierce heavyweight in the coke game and held it down in a major way.

Xav was a street veteran himself and knew everybody who was somebody and all about what they had going on.

He had been deep in the streets since the age of twelve. This in essence, gave him thirty-five years or so of experience in the game. Eight of those being spent in Graterfort State Prison and Camp Hill State Prison.

"Yo, what you got in mind, Capo?" Yammi asked, in reference to the uncle of Khalib and his cousin he had with him, the driver and passenger of the Benz.

"Well, we can't just roll up over there and go shoot 'em up, bang-bang! Besides, I think I like the car. And the nigga Khalib, gonna damn sure pay a ransom for his uncle, because of how much he knows about his operation."

"So, we take the nigga hostage?"

"Facts! Then we get him to lead us to Khalib, and to the money, and to the safes, and to the coke stashes. That's how we gonna handle this," Xav explained.

"I'm with you, yo. I'm with you, no doubt."

Xav had next did the best thing he knew to do. He pulled out his phone and called Roderick, to get his take on all that was happening.

"Yeah, what up, Xav?"

"Bro, check this out, right. Me and my young one, Yammi, we on Broad at the gas station now, and looking on at the nigga Khalib's uncle and his cousin. They washing one of his cars at the detail station. I was thinking about grabbing the uncle and the car? And this will force Khalib to come from wherever he got his ass hiding out, to negotiate a deal to get them back. What you think?"

"That's not even a question, Xav! Do what you gotta do. Snatch the nigga up, and the car, and bring his ass to me! I'll be back around soon. Just put him away until I make my return. Don't worry about the other dude. He might not matter to Khalib. We gonna keep the uncle for ransom though."

"That's exactly what I was thinking, my nigga. I'm out."

They ended the call.

"Yammi, look, I want you to walk over there and kind of ease up close but not look too suspicious to make them niggaz think something. I'm gonna pull up in front of the car and begin talking to 'em to distract them. While they facing me, I want you to pull up behind them and draw down on them niggaz. I'll be stepping out the car by then with my hammer clutched and we lay them niggaz on the ground. I'm gonna force the uncle to the back of my car, once we wrap them nigga's hands and arms behind their backs, and you hop in the Benz and head to the low spot up in northeast. Remember, when we got them niggaz down on the ground, I'mma keep 'em at gun point and you get busy tying they asses up!"

"I got you, Capo! I got you."

The plan was laid. Yammi hopped out and began walking across the street. Xav gave him two pairs of boot laces out the extra pair of *Tims* he kept in his car. They would be used to tie up the hostages.

By the time Yammi made it across the street, Xav was pulling into the drive-thru of the car wash. He rolled down the window then began to talk to them. "Yo! Weed up! Weed up! I got that loud pack!" He caught the attention of both—James, the uncle, and Theo, the cousin—as they were busy washing the car.

Xav gets out his ride and pulled out his pistol, causing them to stop all movement. "Lay the fuck down! Lay the fuck down now, before I start blasting on you bitch-ass niggaz!" he spat.

At first, James and Theo began to slowly back away with their hands in the air. But along came Yammi, to cut off any running room they may had contemplated.

"A'ight-a'ight, nigga! You got it. You got it," James said as they both began to get face down on the pavement.

Once they were tied, Yammi patted them down and got a pistol, a cellphone, the Benz key, and a small knot of cash off James, and a pistol and phone from Theo.

"Get yo bitch-ass up, nigga!" Xav said as he walked over to James, smacking him alongside the face with the heavy metal .357 Magnum he palmed.

Whop!

James was split badly. Blood oozed. Big Xav, a 285-pound nigga; standing at six-foot four in height, snatched James up by the arm, smacked him with the weapon again alongside the face, and splitting him further in the process.

Whop!

The trunk of the Malibu was already opened and Xav pushed James over inside it, once lifting the lid, then slammed it hard to ensure it was locked.

He and Yammi then picked up the pace. Yammi kicked Theo hard in the mouth, dazing him and nearly knocking him out. He hurried and tossed everything he'd gotten off the two to Xav, hopped in the Benz, and peeled off, leaving Theo laid out on the ground bleeding badly at the mouth.

Xav followed through with the plan and they both went in opposite directions. Xav, heading towards Southwest with his kidnapped hostage now who he intended to use for ransom, and Yammi, on the way to the spot in northeast in the big body S-600. He would be able to cap off of it at the chop-shop.

Chapter 16

Geno really began feeling himself these days. So much so to the point that all the interest his uncle Felix had with the group as owners of Seduction City, Geno considered this to be his, as Felix placed him over it, and had himself almost never appeared at the spot to see the operations. His thing was—Felix that is—*so long as his money was correct at the beginning of each month when they did pay-roll, he was perfectly fine. And the nephew, could take care of all the in-between shit them young niggaz had going on. That's why he brought him along for the ride, to do just that,* Felix reasoned in thought.

He and Geno met up at his house one morning to discuss a few things. Geno had motives though. To have his name somewhere on the documents that showed who the rightful owners were.

"Say, unc! I'm glad you was available today, my nigga, for you and me to have this one-on-one as family is accustom to doing."

"My pleasure, nephew. My pleasure. What's on your mind these days, Geno? Me knowing you the way your uncle do, I'm sure you've thought of some big-time plan that'll help advance our purpose, right?" Felix responded.

"You damn right I did, unc! You *damn* right, I do. I've plugged back in with some really important people. And they ready to supply us with all we can handle once again. Likewise, I know without a doubt, that it's time for Geno here, to retake his rightful spot and be the leader I always been known to be."

"And what you getting at, nephew? Shoot it straight with me," said Felix.

"What I'm getting at is this, unc. That goddamn club we got, really belongs to *you* and *me*, unc! Them little young pussy-ass niggaz, ain't doing nothing but using you for ya name, ya license, and ya connections, unc, to do what they do! From what you told me and from what I done found out, they into white collar shit, running scams and the whole-nine! That shit could backfire and fuck around and get you and your name caught up in the mix!" This was intended to be a warning shot to the uncle.

"How you figure though, nephew?"

"How I figured is because it is what it is, unc! I'm there around them niggaz. I hear all they talk about. I see how they having motion and trying to do things. Them niggaz be so busy trying to out do one another, to the point that I wouldn't be nowhere near in surprise, to see a fight breakout between them, and somebody end up getting killed! They got too much of their own shit going on that's keeping them from coming together on the club business. Besides, the background of them niggaz, just don't match our background. And the hustle they still got going on, don't go together with the atmosphere of the club. They using you, unc! They using you! That's all there is to it!" Geno stated emphatically.

He did his best to get Felix to see things in the way he had, that in fact, he was being used by the others, in particular, '*Jamie and that nigga Montell,*' as Geno put it. He was able to peep game and get down to the bottom of what the true objective was of those two.

The conversation continued.

"Geno, how you figure they got bad intentions?"

"Because it's clear, unc. It's very clear. Let me ask you this then, unc, and you tell me. How well you know these dudes?"

"Jamie the only one I know. I don't know anything too much of them other boys,"

"See, my point exactly!" Geno had found an angle to get his uncle to think differently of the guys he was in business with. "That's my point right there. That! You don't know too much about them niggaz at all, to be deeply involved with 'em like you are. They know I'm in there every night, me and Razor. So we see, hear, and know everything them niggaz got going on. And I can't really find out all the facts on them niggaz, because my name ain't nowhere on the paperwork. And I ain't got access into the computer system there, because I ain't got any of the passwords to log-in under," he reluctantly said.

"Computer system?" questioned Felix. He was completely puzzled now.

"Yeah, unc! *Computer system,* nigga! Them suckaz got to keep track of all the activities of the spot, and to hold all the information of the business relations. You see how behind you is compared to them! You too old-school, unc! And too damn slow and outdated to be able to keep up with them niggaz!"

"That's why I got yo ass there, nephew, so you could do all of that for me," Felix reminded.

"But I can't, unc. I ain't got no say-so and no involvement to make a call on how things should go. When them niggaz have conference meetings in the office, I'm not even allowed to be a part of it. But I don't get mad though. I know it's business. It does take a shot at my ego, to be the nigga I am, and have the type of stains in the street I got, to be dictated to by these lil punk-ass muthafuckas' that they is. But I clearly know the tide will change at some point or another. And all I have to do is ride the wave and let it carry me to where it would. But listen, the bottom line is this, unc, you got them niggaz on one side, and then, you got *us*," he gestured with his hand "You, me, and Dirty Harry, on the other. And I for one, don't know how to continue and sit back and let them niggaz run game and get down on me and my people like this. Again, they playing you, unc! And that's just all it is to it! We gotta bring this shit to an end. And soon!"

The nephew was able to get the antiquated uncle of his to be persuaded by his words about the actions that were playing out right before his eyes. Felix had the ultimate leverage, and the larger percentage of the profit the spot turned. Or so he thought on the last part. The only money Montell and company paid out to Felix was the portion he was to get from the entrance fees charged at the door, which was $20 a head, and a small portion from the bar tickets.

Felix didn't know a damn thing about the branding and entertainment profits that were being made. He didn't know about the media dollars that came in from the photography area of the club, videos, the online website memberships that Montell and Jamie wisely thought of and turned a dollar from, or, of the price hiking they had on each bottle of liquor, champagne, or wine sold inside the establishment.

Felix was oblivious to it all. But not Geno. He knew his uncle was being fucked over. But to what degree? He had no knowledge of this exactly. He was, however, determined to get a piece of the pie and eventually make his rise to power. Geno only needed the consent of his uncle to clean up things, then, make his rise back to a position of power.

Felix spoke up again. "Nephew, what you need my permission to do?"

"Unc, listen," he began in answering the question and stood face to face with the brother of his father, "I need for you, to rearrange the paperwork to the spot, to show that *I*, now have a position of ownership with you. And *I* am your liaison in the event anything was to go wrong. Your next of kin, basically. If I'm to be your eyes, ears, and hands at the lounge, then, I need you to let me be that. Because your ass, put me in position there, then tie my hands behind my back. What type of shit do that be about!" Geno expressed.

"Nephew, truth be told on it all, I didn't really think this shit was gonna take off the way it did. I just felt I was returning a big favor to my guy Jamie, when he first came to me about it, due to the favors in the past he's done for me. That's it." Felix let his honestly come out.

"Well, you in it now!" he responded while rolling a joint of weed for he and his uncle to smoke. "And goddamn auntie Pepper got it smelling good as hell in the kitchen," he proclaimed over the aroma of the big breakfast Felix's wife had begun to cook.

Felix smiled at his nephew's comment, then went on with the business talks. "So, you want me to re-do the paperwork, to show you have a stake now with me? And that you, are my agent if something was to go wrong?"

"That's exactly what I need for you to do. And that way, I will have some say-so there, and I'll have access to the system them book smart muthafuckas done put together. Then, from that point, they can't continue to hide shit from us like they doing now. And as I said in the beginning of this conversation, I plugged back in with some really important people, and they ready to supply us with some high-powered shit. All we can handle."

"You know I ain't into that dope dealing, nephew."

"Nigga! What the hell. You ain't! But I am! And we ain't got but one life to live, so you might as well live it. I'm looking to restructure my camp in the same way as I had before, except with a new age twist to it. But just like before, I'm gon' need you to help me hide the work and stash the money. Okay, unc."

"Yeah. We can do that. I need a few extra dollars anyways, to buy me and my wife a nice home out in the suburbs somewhere, away from all the bullshit the inner city has thrown our way. And thanks to you, I'll be able to achieve my goal. The same as last time when I needed the money for the bar, you came through for me then. I really don't know what I'd do without you, nephew."

"Is that right?" Geno remarked. "But what yo ass *could* do is this. Call up a meeting between you and them young niggaz. Let them know what you wanna do. Then, have the proper paperwork written up to make it happen. If they buck on you, then you'll know without a doubt, they got some fuck-shit going on behind your back, unc. But I already know what to expect from them. Trust what I'm telling you. It's the nigga Montell, who seems to be calling all the shots and dictating to them on what to do. The nigga I don't know too much about. But the one who had a lot to say when we first met?"

"Yeah, that nigga! From what I now know, he used to be the leader of their little group before they all got knocked and did time in the feds. And the other nigga, the one you do know of and have dealt with, played second fiddle to Montell. I don't know too much about the other dude though. The quiet nigga. But he don't pose too much of a threat. Not from what I can tell," Felix let out.

"Okay, nephew. You got my blessings to do all you need to do in seeing to it we get our fair share of Seduction City, and our percentage in all the areas money is being made. Besides, I had to pull a 'rabbit out a hat' and go above and beyond, in getting my people down at city hall to grant those permits and increase my alcohol amount on my license. This was despite them niggaz pitching in on the money I needed to butter the palms of my guys. But how soon do I need to set up the meeting to get this party going with your name being in on the paperwork?"

"The sooner unc, the better, the sooner the better. That's all I can tell you," Geno responded, and then puffed the weed twice more before passing to Felix.

They ended the talk, then took a seat at the table to eat the food Felix's wife Pepper prepared for them. They had pancakes, cheese eggs, beef sausage, hash browns, and grits.

Geno then went on about his way to meet up with the guy who was to put him back into the game through his connections. He was a guy who went by the nickname "Brick," but his government was Floyd Thornton. He had ties to a Mexican supplier who provided any amount of the new age drugs that the streets craved; from Meth, E-pills, Molly, you name it, he had it, or could get it, as all was needed from Brick, was to make one call. But Geno's first phase of his mission was taken care of with his uncle, and the plot to slowly move himself into position was working. He burned with fury to gradually rise above the others that was in power, by pushing them out of position and he taking over.

Two

Chapter 17

In Full Hustle Mode...

Montell met with Pete's people. They had the duty to make the delivery of the supply he'd ordered from him. The meeting location took place at a brick home in a seemingly well to do neighborhood in Lithonia, Georgia. The girlfriend Tamron was along with him, in the event any language problem may be there. They had to prevent any misunderstandings from taking place. Also, the transporter of Pete, a guy by the name Javier, was given strict orders, to put Montell and the girl on video call, the very moment they were to arrive.

Pete, wanted to see them and communicate throughout the entire exchange. In addition to Javier being there, he had two of his helpers there as well. They were heavily armed with assault rifles and pistols, and ready to kill on impulse at the word of Javier.

Once Montell and Tamron were escorted from the car— they were told to park in the garage of the home situated on Burnley Lane—into the kitchen, it was time to get down to the business.

"So, you are 'Mo,' correct?" Javier asked.

"Yeah. That be me," dude replied.

In an instance, Javier connected the video for Pete to confirm indeed, it was Mo. They greeted one another.

"So, Mo, my boss there," he pointed to the screen of the laptop, "tells me, I should be expecting one hundred grand in cash from you. Right?" asked Javier again as Pete looked on.

"It's all there," Montell said, then tossed over the mini Gucci duffle bag that had the money in it. There were a thousand $100 bills, nothing else. Javier didn't take Montell's arrogance too well in *throwing* anything to him. But Montell's intentions were good, as that didn't mean anything demeaning or negative by his actions.

Javier opened the bag and saw all the money was there, at least he assumed. On the counter top sat a money machine to count. Javier then pulled out one of those markers to check the money with, to be sure there were no counterfeit bills included.

Now I know damn well this fuckin fool, ain't about to stand there and swipe every single bill in the bag, thought Tamron.

"This is nothing personal, Mo, only business," Javier said.

"No problem, my guy. Take your time," Montell replied.

Tamron then translated his words in Spanish for Javier to clearly understand. He jarred his head as he looked at Tamron in a funny way, once he heard her speak proper Spanish. Pete came over through the video screen to tell Javier what the business was, as he spoke to him in their native tongue himself and then had a laugh. Tamron just smiled. Montell nudged her with his elbow to let her know it was time to let them know, he understood they would be cautious of one another to begin with, but once time progressed and they did more business, no one would be suspicious of the other from that point.

Tamron worded her man's message to them, and the business proceeded.

The money was all calculated and accounted for. A full $100,000. Not one bill short. Montell paid for five kilos of Meth at $10,000 each, and $50,000 for a combination of E-Pills, Molly, Flaka, and so many 500 sheet packets of K-2 laced paper to make strips and ID size portions with. In addition, Pete matched him with a $100,000 worth of the same, so, Montell had double the amount in product. Pete felt the need to lock him in on business. This would obligate Montell in a way. Montell couldn't turn down the offer of consignment, not even if he wanted to.

"Good talking to you, Mo. You now on your way to being a '*Jeffe*' soon," Pete said.

"Thank you. Thank you very much," he responded.

He and Tamron then put the work in the car.

Montell shook hands with Javier. They left, en route to Tamron's house to go through the work and prepare it for retail sales.

The two were on their way to higher status in the world. Montell was now someone he'd never been before in his life, but had always saw others become, a fucking large scale drug dealer. He was about to supply the block.

Chapter 18

Felix eventually made the call for everyone to be present at the lounge for a second meeting, so they could all discuss the business of the day. This took place about two weeks after he and Geno had their conversation about him having some say-so. Everyone who had an interest in ownership showed up for the cause of the OG, Felix.

"It's been a long time since we all had the opportunity to come together and sit down," Felix opened up.

"Yeah, you right, Felix. It has been a long time coming. But nonetheless, we here," Montell was the first to speak up.

"That's right, we here, and it's a good thing," said Jamie.

"Even though we all been busy attending to our own shit in other areas," mentioned Felix, "all of us here today, though."

"What's on your mind, Felix?" Jamie asked. His question caused him, Montell, and Roderick to both look in the direction of Felix, Geno, and Dirty Harry, who stood on the opposite side of the table.

"Well, to begin with, what I have on my mind is this. From this day forward, I wanna pass over fifteen percent of the interest I hold in Seduction City, to my nephew here, Geno," Felix said, and put his hand on Geno's right shoulder. "I wanna let him have the fifteen percent, while me and Dirty Harry, maintain the other twenty percent—ten each," he clarified.

"But here is what I can't seem to understand Felix." Montell formulated his challenge, just as Geno had expected him to do. "Your nephew, Geno there," he pointed at him with his finger, "he was here, or there at your bar, I shall say, (this meeting took place inside Seduction City) when we all first sat down and put this thing of ours together. And you made no mention of any of this then. Why the sudden change now?" asked Montell.

"What explanation should it be, if I'm still operating in the thirty-five percent ownership range?"

"Because it means, now, we gotta go back and re-do the paperwork—add this here, subtract this there—and go out of our way to appease you and compromise the original blueprint. That's why," capped Montell. He was cynical about it.

Felix fired back. "Well, if I own the lion's share of the pie, and was the *main man* to make this here thing come to be, why shouldn't my wishes be respected?"

"Look Felix—"

"Nawl, hold on there, Young-blood!" Felix cut Jamie off with his words, stretching out his hand in gesture and eyeing Montell coldly, awaiting his response. "I wanna hear what your guy there gotta say."

"Real talk, Felix. It's not that your wishes ain't being respected. It's just the point about us having things up and going for weeks now, then, all of a sudden, there comes a special request. One that could potentially shake things up with how we got things going. And not only that. This instant request makes things look *fishy* to me. Plus, we *know* you. We don't know him," Montell spat. His response was directly to Felix. No one else.

"Yo! What you mean, *'that makes things look fishy,'* my nigga?" Geno retorted. He put up a defense for his uncle. "And it ain't for you to know me, homie! I don't know you either! I'm here with my uncle. And have been, for thirty plus years, nigga, as far as business is concerned. I'm *Geno!* BMF *Geno!* Here out the city of ATL! Yeah! Them big facts! City-shit for real, playboy! Check my credentials! And from what I understand unc here," he looked over and pointed at Felix, "don't know you either, or you," he nodded his head to point at Roderick. "He and Jamie know each other. And Jamie was the one who came to him about everything. Seduction City is the idea and work of unc and Jamie. So, it's them two who got all the say-so on how they see things, not you, not me, or him," speaking of Roderick by nodding his head in his direction again. "It's these two right here," Geno made his mark and ended by pointing back and forth at Jamie and Felix.

Things had gotten heated between Geno and Montell in their exchange of words. They both felt the tension between the other. Geno felt satisfied with the fact of putting Montell in his place with his words. And Montell felt offended by Geno coming for him as he had. Especially so since he was on his way to being a street boss, once he put a team together to move his work in the streets and crown him "new boss on the block." But one thing about Montell, he was very good at disguising his emotions and didn't react on impulse to the insult that came from Geno. He simply placed it in the back of his mind and would deal with it at a later date to come.

"Hold up now, fellas, hold up," Dirty Harry intervened, as the slim, baby-faced, slick and wavy haired, raspy voice speaking ghetto veteran, felt the need to defuse the *rah-rah* and the tech between Geno and Montell. "Now the fact of the matter is this. Felix is the senior voice here in the office of the building we all got something to do with, one way or another. And all though we don't see eye to eye on our issues or what-have-you's, we still should be willing to agree to disagree and move forward as business partners," Dirty Harry properly put it.

"You right, you so right, D-Harry. I apologize on all that, Montell. My bad. The best bet is to let my uncle and Jamie talk and we listen, since they're the originators of the idea, and the first two rightful owners," Geno said.

"No problem, Geno. No problem at all, my nigga. What you said just then is the best thing for us to do," Montell responded. He got quiet after that. He knew without a doubt Jamie would make all the decisions and only agree to any terms that would benefit their crew. The one he was a solid member of. All that he, Montell, and Roderick, represented.

"Look Jamie, the reason I wanna do it this way is because as you guys already know, I'm never here. I love being at my bar more than here. That's why I had Geno, be my presence and voice in Seduction City from the get-go. And not only that, I'm too damn old and suffer from ED, to be trying to keep up with you young niggaz, you young-ass bucks, and those fast-ass lil guls that be ripping and running around the place," Felix said, demonstrating with his hand in a downward position and wiggled two fingers back-and-forth like they was a set of legs in motion, "doing what they do to get the fellas to pay top dollar," he further said with his face construed in a funny way, like he was afraid of being eaten alive by a young tender sweetheart.

Everyone laughed at him and the humor of his animation.

"Now, I clearly understand your point, Felix. I clearly do. You too old to be trying to keep up with us younger generation of gangsta niggaz. And your nephew more of our speed," Jamie remarked.

"That's exactly my point."

"I can agree to that, Felix. I can. It's not like Geno don't know anything about what's going on, or ain't had any involvement. He has. And I guess we got to respect your wishes and turnover whatever percentage you looking to empower him with," Jamie said. He came to terms with what Felix asked.

Did that nigga just say 'empower me with?' I think I like his choice of words, with his book-smart ass. Dork-ass, duck-ass, lame-ass, nigga! Geno thought to himself.

"Look Felix, it won't be today, maybe not this week. But in due time, I'm gonna get around to it and make it my business to rearrange the paperwork to be what you want it to be. Then Geno, would hold his rightful position of interest in the group," Jamie said.

"Sounds about right to me, Young-blood. It sho' do," Felix replied.

Montell looked at Jamie in disbelief behind the agreement he'd came to with Felix. It angered him in a way, because he had a strong feeling Geno, had other motivations and designs. He now had the leeway to carry them out in the operations of the club. How he knew? Because his own mind was in the same direction. As the old saying goes, *"Game recognizes game,"* and *"Birds of a feather, does flock together,"* even if they didn't know one another from a can of paint. The body language was identified, and they peeped the intentions of the other. This was the reality that existed between Geno and Montell. Although so distant in personality and demeanor, yet two of a kind in mind and at the heart, rather they knew it or not.

"Rod, what's your take on this?" Montell turned and asked.

"Shit, fine by me. As long as Jamie ain't got a problem making a compromise, I don't have an issue with it. I'm sure Jamie know what he doing, and he got our best interest at heart in any decision he makes. So, I'm cool with it."

"Well, I guess everybody here is in agreement then. Geno, welcome on board as an official owner and interest holder of Seduction City Gentlemen's Night Lounge," Jamie stated, and extended his hand to shake Geno's. They both stretched across the table from where they stood.

Geno fired up a cigar, took a sip of the champagne he had in a glass, then began to speak once more. Montell was still silent. However, he fumed at the agreement of Jamie and Felix. But the negative energy was put away. At least for now.

"Okay, since we got that part out the way, what's the deal on me being given the pass codes to the computer system, so

I can also be able to keep track of the activity of the Lounge and of the business transactions?" Geno inquired.

This nigga ain't had an interest in the group but five seconds, and he already asking for too much too soon. Montell looked at Geno coldly and thought to himself.

Geno's intent was clear. He wanted to put it all out on the table and no longer be in the dark while he had everyone present and seated. He also knew he had to make his move and get them niggaz to ass-up before they got together behind his back and "blackballed" him out the loop, like the owners of the NFL had done to Colin Kaepernick.

"Slow ya roll, 'Speedy Gonzalez!" spat Montell. "We'll get to that point sometime in the near future."

Geno just stared at him and fumed on the inside behind the insult. He then spoke up once more on the subject of the computer system he knew they had established. "I'm sure we will get to that at some point in the near future. I just wanted to make the fact known that *I'm aware.* That's all." he said.

"That's understood, Geno," Jamie chimed in to say. "We definitely plan to update you on all Seduction City got going on."

"—Well, I'm just saying," Geno responded quickly.

Jamie and Montell smiled behind the remark, because it was thought that Geno had no knowledge at all before the day about the system they had functioning. But he did.

"Are we all done here, fellas?" Jamie asked, trying to bring an end to the hour-long meeting.

Everyone looked around at one another to be sure no one had anything further they wanted to say. No one did, and Jamie closed out.

"Felix, it was a pleasure meeting up with you here today and all us coming to an agreement on some things, you and your guys and me and my guys. I appreciate you all on it too, and all y'all be easy," he replied.

Everyone shook hands then left. The time was only 12:45 in the afternoon, and the spot wasn't due to open until 7:00. It was a Thursday.

Chapter 19

Geno went and got in his car where his driver and personal friend Razor was waiting. He had texted earlier to come pick him up. Once seated, he began to tell Razor all about what was discussed, and about the heated exchange him and the new nemesis—Montell—went through. Razor laughed at it, because Geno, pretty much predicted how things were to go. This was hours beforehand.

"Say Geno, you did say of all them, it would be the nigga named Montell, to cause the most problems or go the hardest in challenging you," Razor said.

Geno just continued to shake his head as he thought back over the entire meeting and the words that came out of Montell's mouth.

"And you know something else too, Razor? The nigga had the nerve to reveal exactly how much he don't like me, with all the sarcastic shit he was on. I didn't like it at all, man. I didn't like that shit! Some country-ass nigga, so-called himself popping off at me, bruh! We may bump heads at some point in the future," he said, as they continued to talk and ride, heading to a fast-food joint to get something to eat.

Felix and Dirty Harry talked over a few things themselves as well, as they were en route first to the bar Dirty Harry owned, so he could get his car, then, he would meet up with Felix later in the day at his spot.

Montell, Jamie, and Roderick, all went their separate ways. Jamie placed a call to the lawyer who processed the paperwork for them on the club. He let him know that in due time, there would be a need to rearrange a few clauses in the contract. Didn't necessarily say when. Only expressed "in due time." The attorney advised to just let him know and he was on it.

Roderick was now in preparation to take a flight back home to Philly the next day, so to attend to the business that needed his attention.

Big Xav was now his next in charge. He held things down. But didn't want to make too many decisions on issues without Roderick having an input.

Just a day ago, Xav and one of his soldiers, snatched up the uncle of the enemy, and beat down the cousin of the dude that called the hit that ended the life of Roderick's brother. And they were looking to settle the score one way or another—them or the dudes from the other side. Either way, somebody's got to die. And more bodies were about to drop.

***

There were two stops Montell needed to make. The first was to the bank to meet up with Mandy and ensure all the accounts he needed set up were completed. He lied to her by saying the accounts and all the transactions that were to pass through them, would be on legitimate grounds, which was partially true. But the money was to be forwarded to Pete. Once he was to leave there, he would then go to Tamron's house, and they both would begin to package up the drug supply into additional baggies for retail. This was the product he had not long gotten from Javier, Pete's guy, only a few days ago.

Tamron had four female friends she wanted to utilize to help get rid of the dope they had. And Montell, had a few dudes himself, he wanted to supply and put on in the game. But it was the girlfriend—Tamron—who saw the grand opportunity to really take charge of all she and Montell had going on. She felt by her holding a position in the shadows and not stepping into a leadership role—the position of a "boss-bitch" she thought herself to be—stagnated her growth and prevented the power moves she should have been took the initiative to make.

Her time was at hand. She was sure to keep in mind the words of her uncle—the police detective on the Atlanta force. He said to her, *"if and when she was to ever make a decision to get involved in any illegal activities, to simply let him know."* His thing was, he wanted to teach, guide, and protect her, to the best of his ability. He knew all about the lust and attraction she had, to powerful, dangerous, and criminal-minded dudes. He promised her father and her he would do as he say he would. *"With his life on it."* And to prove this, he took a blood oath with his brother Leon. This was Tamron's father.

At the thought of those words, she pulled out her phone and made the call to the uncle to talk about nothing else but her intentions.

He answered, "Hey Tamron! How you?"

"I'm good, Uncle Leroy. I am. And I'm also ready to finally have that sit down to talk with you on a few things. I really am."

Chapter 20

Back In Philly...

Big xav smacked James across the head once again with the .357 Magnum. He was trying to force him to talk. He'd been chained at the ankles and tied up for the past week and barely alive. The takers awaited Roderick's return to Philly.

Xav only gave James a cup of Ramen noodle soup and two 20-ounce bottles of water one time daily. This was just enough to keep him alive, to possibly reveal where the money, the coke, and his nephew were. The only words Xav and Yammi got out of their hostage was "fuck you,"

kiss my ass," and "suck my dick, y'all bitch-ass niggaz!" Ultimate insults

Khalib had a strict rule for any and everyone who was a part of his heroin enterprise, no matter what, *"do not give in and do not give up! It's death before dishonor, and no one was above the code."* Not even Khalib himself. But truth be told, James didn't really know too much about the cash spots of his nephew's fortune, nor of the locations of the drug stashes. The only thing Xav would be able to get James to do was get Khalib on the phone. But before Xav was to force him to make the call, he wanted to wait for Roderick to get back from Atlanta. That day arrived.

Roderick was contacted and told to come alone to the low-key house in Southwest Philly. This was one of the brother A-One's houses.

Xav had James caged in like a stray dog in an animal shelter. He was literally locked in a kennel in the basement of the home.

Roderick arrived. "So, what we got here?" asked Roderick.

"This nigga right here, baby boy, is the uncle to the nigga who had your people killed," Xav let him know.

"Drag that bitch-ass nigga out here at my feet!"

Xav opened the gate to the cage (he had on gloves) and gripped James by the ankles, then pulled him out to the open area.

Roderick looked down on him scornfully, then kicked him in the face, and spit on him.

Shaking and near crying, James attempted to speak and maybe convince the three ruffians—Roderick, Big Xav, and Yammi—he didn't have shit to do with anything, that he's a guilt-free man, and to spare him his life. They weren't hearing none of that shit he had to say.

"Please y'all. Please. I'm begging you, please. Don't kill me. Don't. I don't know nothing my nephew got going on. I'm just a runner. I wash his cars, feed his dogs, and put up with his shit year-round. I don't know nothing about nobody getting killed," James pleaded.

"Nigga! My muthafuckin' brother and my cousin dead! Not to mention the other guy my brother had with him. And you talking 'bout, *don't kill you!*" Roderick spat and kicked him again. "Where this nigga phone at, Xav?"

"It's right here." Xav then gave him James's device.

"Turn that muthafuckin' phone on, nigga, and get your nephew on the line now!"

James held the power button on the device and about five seconds later, it powered to life. The inbox was flooded with a shit load of text messages and voicemail notifications from Khalib, wanting to know what happened and where he was. He also wanted to know about the car of his. Theo recovered and made it to him to let him know everything.

James drew out the pattern on the security screen lock and the phone lit up with the apps.

"Call your nephew, nigga. And put the speaker on," barked Roderick. He turned aggressive and gangsta now! A major step up from being the quiet schoolboy who wouldn't pop shit for nothing! Not even gum! Not even a brown paper bag with air in it in the cafeteria of his high school or college.

The murder of his brother and cousin was challenging on his emotions. Not to mention the growing pain of having to take over the drug operation of A-One's and all that came along with it. This, of course, was in combination with Roderick being pissed off at himself for being a failure in academics. It all brought out the worst in him. His heart turned black and hard. Of all people in their family, it was Roderick, who was now super-ready to kill somebody. On the real, he was.

Khalib's phone rang. He answered. "Yo! Unc! Where you at?"

"Nephew, they still got me. They got me. They wanna speak to you," James told him.

"Khalib!" spoke Roderick.

"Yo, who the fuck you be?" Khalib shouted into the phone.

"I'm gonna be your worst muthafuckin' nightmare, nigga, if you don't come clean about something!"

"What!!" Khalib responded.

"Look, you bitch-ass nigga! I ain't in the business of repeating myself! So, I'mma just go ahead and get to the point, a'ight! You took two people away from me and my family over some petty street shit. My brother, and my cousin—"

"Yeah! And you next, nigga, if you don't cut my uncle loose and give me back my car!" Khalib vehemently spat.

"So, this how we gonna do this? This what you want, nigga? You want head for head? Body for body?" An eye for an eye and a tooth for a tooth, nigga?" Roderick said.

"Yeah, nigga, is that what you want?" Big Xav spoke out.

"Shit, if this how it gotta be, this how it's gotta be! You call it how you see it. Because ain't no compromising on my end! Unc already know the rules. Ain't no negotiations! So, if you feel like you want this beef to never end, then do what you do. And me and my squad, gonna do what we do. So, don't think you gonna hold my uncle and my car for ransom. I ain't coming off shit, nigga!" Khalib capped.

"Fair enough, soldier," Roderick said and grabbed the revolver from Big Xav. "That's fair enough! You said a mouth full then!"

Bang! Bang-Bang-Bang-Bang-Bang!

Roderick shot James multiple times, once in the forehead, and five times about the upper body. He picked up the phone and said one last thing to Khalib.

"Game on, fuck-nigga!" He then slammed out the phone and took the battery from it, and the SIM card.

Big Xav and Yammi looked on at him in total shock, not truly believing that it was Roderick, the madman dressed in casual clothes and a former schoolboy that was doing this. The image did not match up to the actions.

Roderick handed Xav back his gun. "Y'all clean this mess up for me, okay. I'll catch up with y'all later, maybe tomorrow," he said to the other two squad members.

"We got it, Rod. We here," Xav replied. He noticed Roderick get teary eyed.

He looked Xav straight in the eyes. "I appreciate you too, bro, and you too Yammi," he thanked them, then turned to walk out and leave them to do their work on cleaning up the crime scene and getting rid of the body. James was Roderick's first murder victim.

Chapter 21

After The Fact...

Roderick kept situated in Philly for a time being and was busy getting things in order with the street team he'd inherited at the death of his brother. They were war ready at the same time, in the event Khalib and company, was to retaliate behind the kidnapping and whacking of his uncle.

He and his sister Lea was in her car together on their way to Atlantic City, to do a little gambling and maybe enjoy a boxing match or two while there. Big Xav and his cousin, J-Rock, followed behind Xav's truck. They too, were into poker tables and slot machines, and loved the culture and sport of boxing. Besides, their hometown Philly, is considered "fight town USA."

The time was about seven P.M. Lea's cellphone rang. It was a number she'd become all too familiar with. It was their cousin, someone who was doing fed time for conspiracy. He had twenty years to serve. Things were somewhat easy on his end though, as he had a cellphone himself, a very valuable piece of contraband for an inmate, in fed or State.

"Yeah, what it do, cuz," Lea answered.

"I'm good Lea. I'm good. What you up to?" Josh asked.

"I'm on my way to AC, me and Rod," she replied.

"Oh, Rod home?"

"Yeah, bro here—"

"What up, Josh," Roderick greeted him, as Lea had him on speakerphone.

"What's good, fam! Long time, baby boy. It's been a long time, ain't it," Josh stated.

"Hell yeah, it has been. It's been a long time coming. Where they got you at now?"

"Man, these dicks got a nigga way out here in Cali, cuz. I'm at USP Victorville."

"Oh, they got you in Cali! Shit sweet out there or what?" Roderick asked, as he wanted to know what the contraband movement was talking about. This was in the event if he needed to put a something together for his cousin to get himself a pack in his hand and begin seriously having motion from behind the wall.

Josh did have people who were willing to drop for him.

"Yeah, for the most part. I got this Spanish bitch I'm working with out here. It won't be too much longer though, before I finally lock her in like I wanna," Josh responded.

"You say you *where*?" Roderick asked again.

"I'm in Victorville. Out in Cali, cuz," Josh repeated.

"Oh. I ain't never go out west when I was doing my time. They had me in South Carolina and in Mississippi. Wait. *Where* nigga?" The name of the city "Victorville," triggered something in his memory, causing him to ask for a third time.

"Victorville, nigga! You crazy or something, cuz! Why you asked that the way you do?"

"It ain't nothing, cuz. I'm really just trying to remember, why do the name *'Victorville,'* stand out in my mind the way it do. That's all," Roderick said.

"Maybe because you been doing time in fed lock-up, Rod. This muthafucka' biting out here too, boy! You hear me! Shit always popping off! Just last week, some *'Ghostface'* white boy got hit up by his own peeps. He was whacked outright! They caught him down bad with his dick in the ass of a nasty-ass *'Shamoone','* Josh related

"Boy stop! No-he-wasn't!" Roderick responded.

"Oh yes the fuck he was too! They popped that fuck-boy who he was with too, fam! He lived though. Miraculously.

He got another chance to suck on more dicks in the future, once they finally let his faggot-ass off PC," said Josh.

I knew it had to be something. I think I remember what it was now. I'mma call my nigga Montell, to be sure about this shit, Roderick thought to himself.

"Cuz. Me and Lea gonna call you right back in a minute, alright. You on a jack, right?"

"Yeah, I am."

"Okay, that's a bet. We gonna hit you right back shortly. I got to make a quick call," he said as he attempted to rush off the phone before he lost the thought he had.

Josh let them know he would call back shortly and Roderick disconnected. He then pulled out his own phone to make a call.

"Yeah, what up, Rod," the person on the other line answered.

"Yo Mo. I got something I wanna ask you."

"What's that, bruh?"

"I was just talking to one of my cousins in the feds, and he say they got him out in Victorville, Cali. What's so familiar about the name? I can't quite remember?"

"Victorville, Cali? Oh. That spot! You remember the time when I first got out and we was at my spot, I pulled it up on the phone one day looking to locate somebody. That's the spot where they got that bitch-ass nigga, Rico at!"

"I knew it was something! That's what it was. I couldn't remember right off, but now that you reminded me, that's what it was."

"And you say you got a cousin out there at the same spot?" Montell asked for clarity.

"Yeah. A live wire too, boy! You hear me! Cuz wit the fuck shit!"

"Well, shit, I'm sure you already know where I'm going with this and what to do."

"You got to know I do, Mo. You got to. But check, let me hit you back shortly. I got to get in touch with my people again and find out do he know of the nigga or able to locate what dorm he in."

"That's what's up. And in the meantime, I'm gonna go back online to be sure Rico still at the same spot. I'll text you the answer."

"Already, Mo."

"Already, Rod," Montell replied and they ended the call.

"Lea, hit Josh back for me. I wanna relate something to him," he instructed his sister to do so as they cruised down the Atlantic City Expressway, just outside of Egg Harbor Township.

"Yeah, what up Lea," Josh answered.

"Say Josh, bro wanted to holla at you on some important shit," she said and took the phone off speaker to minimize herself knowing the details of their business. Roderick got the phone from her and he and Josh began talking.

"Cuz," Roderick began.

"Talk to me, Rod."

"Listen, if I'm not mistaken, it's a nigga out there by the name 'Rico Locus,' from ATL. You familiar with the name?"

"Yeah, I done heard of him many times, if this the same one. A loud-mouth bragging-ass nigga, who love to talk shit about sports. Nigga love those sorry ass Atlanta Falcons too!" Josh said.

"That's him, fam. Yeah, that's him. How you know the nigga so well though, Josh?"

"Rod, you know I fuck with the sports betting shit heavy. And Rico, is the nigga who run the 'Parlay' and the 'Pool' up in here. He one of the main dudes who do this. He don't go by 'Rico' no more though, I don't think. Everybody call him 'Blue Dot Loc.' He 'Eight-Tre Gangsta Crip' now. The nigga got some rank in that gang shit too, cuz," Josh revealed.

Roderick's phone vibrated. He looked at the screen. It was Montell. The text message he sent read:

MONTELL: *Rat-ass nigga still there!*

RODERICK: *Mo, I'm about to hit you back in a minute. This shit serious bro!*

Roderick then continued to talk with Josh, as he was seated in the passenger space of the car and Lea pushed the BMW 5-series down the highway, a car A-One bought for her before he was killed.

"What's so special about the nigga Blue Dot, cuz?" Josh asked.

"Josh, the nigga is the reason me and the crew down in Georgia went to prison to begin with!"

Lea turned her head swiftly to look at Roderick, as she couldn't believe what was just said. She fixed her eyes back towards the road ahead and continued to mind her own business and didn't comment on the conversation they were discussing.

"Cuz, you got to be bullshitting me, ain't you! You got to be. As much rank and as much pull that the nigga got in that gang shit, I know damn well, that nigga 'Blue Dot,' didn't eat no cheese and rat on a nigga!" Josh expressed in a disbelieving tone of voice, being he saw Rico on a daily basis conduct and carry himself like a boss and the OG that he *was*.

"So, what? You mean to tell me, Rico, done got down with a gang—"

"—And got rank with it, cuz!" Josh let out before Roderick could finish his sentence.

"Them niggaz don't do background checks on muthafuckas' before they welcome them in?" Roderick asked, as he seemed to know how the process was *supposed* to go.

"Apparently not," Josh remarked.

"Look cuz. I got all the paperwork on this nigga, written statements and all. And not only that, I got my homies down in Atlanta, who took the fall along with me behind the nigga Rico snitching."

"So, what exactly do you need me to do, cuz? Let's get straight to the point, shall we," Josh stated seriously, as he knew his cousin had a reason as to why he related all he had to him about this individual.

"Real talk, I need you to expose that bitch-ass nigga for who he really is! Then, once he has no more help and support, I need you to make a move on him, if them Crip niggaz don't pop that pussy first, before you and yo squad do, you hear me!"

"Enough said, cuz. I'mma handle that ASAP! How soon could you get the paperwork to me?"

"I can send you an email of it, and mail you the actual paperwork next week, straight from my lawyer."

"Okay, bet! You do that. I'mma go ahead and get busy tryna find out who over the nigga in rank that's here and bring it to their attention about this ratting shit."

"Yeah, cuz, that's what you do. Get on top of it" Roderick directed, and the two ended the call.

Roderick then called Montell back to let him know all that was said between him and his people. Montell couldn't believe his ears about Rico being part of a gang now. He figured Rico had thought over everything, and knew he needed to think up a good way to manipulate his reality, in order to save his own ass from being killed.

How did that happen? Montell thought to himself after the call from Roderick. But it was what it was, and it was going to be what it's going to be. The important thing for them was that they now knew that Rico was no longer on PC, and that he could be touched by a hired goon when need be. If only 'Jimmy Smack' and his people knew what the deal was. Niggaz would be taking aim at Rico's head from both angles, or even a third one, once them Crip cats get knowledge of what he was all about. He—Rico—was a pussy and a rat! A *Tom* and *Jerry* ass nigga, all in one.

Chapter 22

Roderick and Lea, along with Big Xav and the guy who rode with him, finally made it to AC. They first went to see a boxing match at Bally's Casino resort. The main event was between two middleweights. It was a non-title 10 round bout.

As they were leaving the arena to go towards the gambling floor, Roderick caught a glimpse from the corner of his eye, some dude who looked very familiar to him. The guy was walking with a Spanish female. If Roderick didn't know any better, he'd thought the waffle-colored light skin dude he looked on at, was the NBA star, Steph Curry. And at the same time, of all the people he knew personally, only one of them, who actually resembled the basketball star in many ways, and that was his former friend but now foe, for the betrayal and disloyalty he'd committed. This was Eric. It had to be Eric Tyree Mickens.

Is that who I think it is? Roderick questioned himself. As he inched closer upon the crowd heading towards the double doors that separated the casino floor from the showroom floors. He saw the one thing that indeed confirmed that it was Eric, the tattoo of a ferocious-looking predatory bird on the left side of his neck. It was the image of an African Secretary bird.

As they entered the casino, the fly Spanish female who was with Eric, paused momentarily to get a drink from one of the servers. And at this, it allowed Roderick and Lea the time necessary to catch up and approach. Lea knew nothing about who Eric was, nor of the animosity that existed between her brother and the waffle-colored guy. All she knew was, her sibling was angry about something and was stepping to some dude to get something off his chest.

"What's good E," Roderick said to get the attention of Eric. He was slightly startled by the sudden roar of the voice, as it had registered in his mind who it belonged to. At the point of the guy turning to find out who was behind him, no doubt, Roderick called him right out. It was Eric. "Long time, nigga!" Roderick spat.

"Yeah, what's good," Eric stated in reply, and looked deep into the eyes of Roderick. He thoroughly searched his face for any signs of aggression. None discovered, and he stood in one space and continued in silence awaiting the next words to come out the mouth of Roderick.

"So, that's how you do your homie, my nigga? You run off with all his money. You smashed his girl. You get her pregnant. Then, you go ghost without being found. Not until now, at least. What part of the game is that, yo!" Roderick said to Eric with a bit of anger in his voice.

Eric took a long pause before responding. "I don't owe nary one of you niggaz an explanation about any of my business," he said and turned to walk off.

"Yo nigga! You don't disrespect my muthafuckin' brother like that! What the fuck is wrong with you! Ol' nut-ass nigga!" Lea spat. Eric kept calm and continued to walk, with Roderick and Lea on his heels.

"Yo Eric! I'm talking to you, nigga. How the fuck you gone do Montell and us like that, and think shit gonna be alright? Nigga, you do owe us an explanation! What the fuck wrong with you!" Roderick spat, obviously in more anger than he was only twenty seconds before. Remember: he was a killer now. Shit was all serious with dude.

Eric stopped once more to address him. "Like I said, I don't owe nobody any explanation about my muthafuckin' business. And that's that, partner!"

140

Lea looked at him in total anger. Her mode switched from subtle to pit bull. And she was ready to smack the fuck out of Eric at Roderick's orders to do so.

Joleena finally spoke up. "Eric, what is going on between you and *these* people here?" she questioned. She had a bit of snobbishness to her statement and her face displayed a strong form of disdain and scorn.

"Yo, all you gotta do is keep quiet and only speak when spoken to, shorty!" Lea warned her.

"Just be cool, Joleena. Everything's all right," Eric said to her, as he knew of the temper Lea had, and thought over some of the stories Roderick once told the crew of the cat fights Lea had been the winner of.

"Nigga, you know that's some bullshit you pulled, don't you! Roderick spat. You and the warden bitch, running off on Montell with all the paper that man had. That's some foul shit, dude. You violated in a major way, my nigga. Had you not took off with the *Scrilla*, I don't think it would be a problem. I'm sure Montell wouldn't care if you housed the bitch. But the *Scrilla*—that paper you stole—was the area where you went wrong at, nigga. And not only did you take from him, you took from us too, you bitch-ass nigga!"

"Yo! Watch that mouth, dude! Don't you got any class and respect for the women in our presence? You still ghetto ass fuck, Rod! The typical gutter-ass dirty Philly nigga!" Eric insulted.

"What, nigga!

Eric then grabbed Joleena by the hand and began to walk off, because he knew Roderick was stung badly by the insult and would react off impulse had he continued to stand in front of him.

I know what to do. Roderick thought to himself, then pulled out his iPhone to *FaceTime* Montell, as he and Lea slowly walked behind Eric and Joleena, as they headed to an area where slot machines were.

"Yeah, what it do, Rod," Montell answered

"Yo Mo. Me again. And boy, you ain't gonna believe who the fuck I'm walking behind right now, my nigga? I ran into this bitch-ass nigga right here in AC."

Montell knew without a doubt, it had to be somebody Roderick didn't like, for him to call someone out of their name in insult. But he never thought for once it would be Eric he was referring to.

"Who that you talking about, Rod?" he wanted badly to know.

Roderick hit the icon to rotate the camera on the phone.

"This nigga right here," he spat, as he had the camera trained on Eric and Joleena.

Montell strained his eyes to make out exactly who it was, but had confirmation once Eric turned to see what Roderick had going on.

"That's that fuck-nigga Eric, ain't it? Ain't that's that pussy-nigga, Rod?"

"Yeah, that's the nigga! It's him. Talking about he don't owe nobody no explanation on his business or on what he did to you."

"What!"

"Yeah, Mo, that's what the bitch-ass nigga said."

"Aye man, I ain't gonna be too many more of your bitch niggaz, yo! You got that!" Eric stopped, turned, and said angrily.

"Nigga, you'll be whatever the fuck my brother say you are! With yo bitch-ass! Pussy-boy!" Lea cut in and spat.

"Baby, what is going on here?" Joleena exclaimed, now demanded to know.

"Yo nigga you got there, foul as shit, shorty! The nigga cutthroat. He conniving. And he a slimy-ass nigga!" Roderick said to Joleena about her boyfriend.

Joleena looked at Eric, then at Roderick, and again at Eric to wait on his reply to the words of Roderick.

"You know what Joleena, let's go. We can find another spot to enjoy ourselves with no interference," Eric said and began walking to the exit.

"Eric, you pussy-ass nigga! You a bitch! A bitch, you hear me! You and that slimy bitch, Verena! You and that nasty hoe, done ran off with my muthafuckin' money! And you nigga! You! I trusted you, E! How you do me like that? Run off with my girl and my money! Now that's foul my nigga. Foul!" Spat Montell.

Chapter 23

Eric turned and veered into the screen of the phone to make eye contact with Montell. He said to him. "What more could I say, MO. Shit happens. Shit happens, my guy," he spat, turning and continued to walk, he and Joleena. She had a concerned look about her face. A small level of fear came over her.

Roderick and Lea continued to follow the couple to the parking lot. He spat insults and other disrespectful vernaculars. Eric didn't react impulsively. He kept his cool. In fact, he or Joleena, didn't utter another word. They just continued to walk.

Roderick definitely wanted to do something to Eric, since he had him directly in his sights. But what? He couldn't draw a pistol and shoot him. Nor could he point one to threaten him. Besides, his gun was too far away locked in the car. Roderick's intent was to see what the car looked like Eric drove and get his tag number. He could possibly connect with somebody that work at a police department or the DMV, pull up the information the car was registered in, and get the home address.

"Yo, Lea, when we get to to the car where they walking to, I want you to take a picture of the tag and the car, okay," Roderick whispered to his sister.

"I got you bro."

Yo Mo, I'mma hit you back in a minute, a'ight," he said to Montell. He was still on video call.

"That's a bet, Rod. You do that, my nigga."

They ended the call.

Eric and Joleena made it to the car with Roderick and Lea still following. He opened the passenger door for Joleena. She got in and locked the door behind herself. As Eric attempted to walk around the rear of the car to go towards the driver's side, Roderick and Lea blocked his path.

"Yo nigga, what the fuck you want with me? My business ain't got shit to do with y'all no more. What part about that not clearly understood? Eric said to Roderick as they stood face to face and starred one another down. Then, Eric tried to pass, but Roderick put up his arms and stopped him. He froze in place, looked down at Roderick's hand pressed on his chest, had a look up into his face again, and knocked his arm down aggressively off him. Roderick pushed him hard. This triggered a vicious anger from Eric. He didn't hesitate to react. He took off on Roderick by punching him square in the face.

The blow dazed Roderick badly. He hadn't expected Eric to be the tough guy he'd turned out to be. Lea began to fire off on Eric to allow her brother the time to regain his composure and they could get on Eric's ass like they wanted to. But Eric proved to be more than they could handle in this particular instance. He grabbed Lea by the arm, around the bicep area, and slung her little one hundred and twenty pound-self crashing headfirst into the SUV that was parked next to his car, knocking her out cold.

Eric then rushed Roderick and began to put a flurry of blows on the guy, along with a knee to the face that busted his lips.

Roderick managed to get to his feet and grabbed Eric, holding him until his vision cleared up and he was able to go at it in a more effective way. Lea eventually recovered and was attempting to get to her feet, but it was a case of too little, too late. Security made it to them and began to hose everybody down with pepper spray. Roderick was still holding on to Eric and biting him on the right shoulder until the effect of the spray took over and caused all three of them to choke and cough badly.

"Get down on the ground, now! Get down! The casino security guards began to bark at the participants of the squabble.

They all were coughing badly from the spray, as the security team moved in to cuff them. Defeated, they reluctantly lay to the pavement.

Joleena, stepped out the car to try and let the police know exactly what went on, that they were followed by the boy and the girl—Roderick and Lea—that she didn't know their names; and that, her and her boyfriend, were innocent. But before she could get close enough to the arresting guard who she *thought* looked friendly enough to hear all she had to say, the guard that happened to have cuffed Lea, a separate guard rushed her and shot a stream of spray directly in her face, causing Joleena to drop to the concrete and go into a severe asthma attack. Lea began to laugh and talk shit to her in her moment of having a health crisis.

"*Ahhh-haaa*! You wannabe high-class bitch! Die already!" Lea spat. She'd recovered from her moment of being knocked out.

Roderick, Eric, and Lea, all went directly to jail, while Joleena was rushed to the hospital to be treated. The charges? Disorderly conduct, fighting in public, and assault and battery. Their bail was sky high. Joleena would suffer the same fate once she was to recover and be released from the hospital.

When the Atlantic City PD took over on the arrest, they thought that the fight was between two couples, being there was a group of a male and female on both sides. But that wasn't the case.

As bad as Eric didn't want to, he had to call Verena to come post bail for him. He knew without a doubt there would be no end to her words, especially not so behind the fact she now knew he had been in AC with another woman. And she had to pay to get his car out the impound while she was there to post his bail.

Joleena, called her cousin, Caitlin, to come bail her out. She couldn't afford to have her father or her brothers know anything about what went on, as they would definitely condemn Eric then, and prevent her from seeing him ever again. She told Caitlin all about the ordeal.

Roderick had his people to quickly come get him and Lea. But she did managed to snap a photo of the license plate too, by the way. And of the car. The plan was to track down Eric and Verena and know their place of residence, so to let Montell know about it. But in this too, Eric created an additional enemy in Roderick with the fight. Roderick now wanted smoke. With his new-found power, he wanted to put it to good use by having a hit placed on Eric's head.

Speaking of Eric, he and Verena, had the roughest argument they'd ever had once they got home. Verena's mother needed to intervene. That's just how loud and outrageous they'd gotten. It was messy.

Eric stormed out the house yet again, and went to go try to make things right with Joleena, since he had went into business with her family now through her brother Robert. He had to make it right again. His narcotics dealings depended upon it.

Chapter 24

Tamron was at the house of her police detective uncle and discussing a few important things with him on the business her and Montell had going on. She knew when it really came down to it, the only true person in her corner, as it related to her being involved in illegal dealings and protection, was her uncle Leroy, the fearless cop.

"So, what you got so important nowadays to talk with your uncle about, TeeTee?" he asked. He and Tamron sat in the den section of his home.

"Well, you know you've always told me about the promise to keep you vowed to my daddy, right?

"Yeah. Okay."

"So, me and my boyfriend wanna Play in the game for a little while now. The money and the opportunity is just too irresistible, uncle Leroy. This dude I'm with now, is in the big league."

"Tee Tee, please don't tell me you got you another one of those little penny-ante ass street punks in your life again, do you? One who's pump-faking like he's the man, but really just a shrimp!" the uncle responded. "I've bailed you out of too many petty situations in the past to continue in letting you go on this way."

"Oh no-no-no, Uncle Leroy. This ain't another *Young Quan*, a *Lil B*, or a *Trey-So* situation I've gotten myself into. This guy here is far more connected than they ever was. The only reason you just now hearing about him is because he's been in Federal lock-up for several years and just got free not too long ago."

"So, he's an ex-con too?" Leroy retorted.

"Yes, yes, he is. But there's an upside to it. While in the Feds, he met a guy whose family is a part of a Colombian cartel. Everything is official too. *Everything,* Uncle Leroy."

"How so?" he asked, interest now perked up.

"Because if it wasn't, I wouldn't be here trying to broker a deal with you to protect him and me."

"You dead-ass serious too, ain't you, TeeTee," the uncle remarked once detecting she really meant business this time, and didn't intend to play any games.

"Uncle Leroy, I am. I most definitely am," she responded, then crossed her legs very lady like and elegantly. She was well situated in a $3,000 Fendi dress and $1,300 heels. The tote bag she clutched in her lap had about $40,000 in it, with $25,000 at the ready to go to her uncle. She leaned back in her seat, flipped her $3,500 weave a few times, then put on a very business-minded type expression about her face and said to her uncle, "So you ready to talk business or what, Uncle Leroy?"

The uncle was taken aback by the confidence his niece showed, so he knew from that point forward, he needed to quit with the bullshit and get down to business.

"Let's get down to business, TeeTee. Let's do that," he stated. "Talk to me. What you got going on?" he asked, and the negotiations began.

"Yeah let's do this, shall we," commented Tamron, then pulled out a stack of cash. "This right here, is for you. The initial deposit from me and my man," she said while extending the cash offer. He looked at her in astonishment. There was a long pause as the uncle knew the moment he was to accept money, he would be obligating himself to them, and it was to be strictly business from there.

Leroy cracked a half smile then leaned forward to get the cash. He popped the thick rubber band that secured the dough and began to count it, licking his right thumb and index finger.

"That's twenty-five thousand there, Uncle Leroy."

"It is? I see now you really ain't bullshitting, are you. But tell me what the business is," he stated.

"Okay, Uncle Leroy. The business is this. My boyfriend used to be into doing white collar things—tax scams, credit cards, travelers checks, mortgage fraud, white collar shit—but not no more too much. The guy he connected with, gave him all the information he needed to contact his people down in Colombia. This of course is at the point of him being ready to go to the big league," she revealed.

"Um-hmm. I'm listening," he acknowledged.

"Okay, so, when my boyfriend reached out to the people down in Colombia, the brother of the incarcerated friend, they had a video conference call to discuss the business and eventually negotiate a deal."

"Okay, so, where do *you* come into play at? How are you tied into this, other than being the girlfriend of a guy, that is?"

"Actually, I play the most important role for my boyfriend. I have to do all the translating for him to the connect in Colombia, because the guy's English not too well."

"Oh! So, you know *all* the business, and it won't be any business, if you not speaking for your dude?"

"Exactly! He needs me more than he *thought* he would, at the time he first reached out and touched the one in Colombia."

"I assume you were a part of that conference call?" he asked.

"Uncle Leroy, I *was* the conference call. I did most of the talking. I believe I made a good impression on the Colombian connect. He seemed to be impressed. He actually thought I was Latina, because of how well versed and fluent

I am with the language." Tamron felt proud of herself to relate.

"Is that right. I guess all the private schooling your daddy and momma put you through turned out for the best."

"It must have. Especially those Spanish classes," she stated and looked at her uncle crack a congratulating smile at the moves she'd positioned herself to be in.

Leroy took the money to the bedroom the niece paid him. While in there, he grabbed one of his cellphones, activated the audio recording system, put the phone on his hip, and returned to the den where she awaited.

The conversation continued, "So, if any, what moves have you two made with the guy down in Colombia so far?" he asked.

"We made a move already. This boyfriend of mine had me really fooled. I'm thinking this nigga was gonna be broke getting out of prison. But to my surprise, how 'bout this muthafucka had a hundred-thousand dollars tucked away somewhere! Probably more."

"So, the boyfriend got it like that, huh?"

"I told you, Uncle Leroy. The bastard was heavy into the white-collar shit for years before they got caught."

"*They?*" he asked.

"Yeah. He got a group of guys he tight with."

"I understand now. But the hundred thousand dollars you mentioned he had. What did he do with it?" dude wanted to know. He'd was recording the second portion of their conversation now. Essentially performing the work that a detective would do, *investigations.*

"Yeah, the loot was spent with the connect. He matched him too in product on consignment," she informed.

"Did he? And the product of choice you and your man now into selling?"

"Uncle Leroy, *all* the party drugs are the most popular, you know, Meth, E-Pills, Xans, and pure cocaine. We got put on for real. Now that my man and his boys, got a new club up and going, we got a good way to clean the money and make it legit."

"Oh, so your boyfriend part owner of a club too, huh? Which one?"

"The new strip club that opened not too long ago over in Fourth Ward—Seduction City the name of it," she related.

"I've been hearing some nice things about that spot. But about the service you looking for me to do for you and the boyfriend. Exactly how much product do y'all got access too?" He wanted to know specifics. "I need to know these things, so I'll be aware of how much protection would be necessary. You know the more money you make, the more problems you subject to have. You got robbers, killers, and envious drug dealers out there in the world, TeeTee. And these muthafuckin' monsters will take aim and gun you down, if you ain't properly protected. But I got a team of dudes myself I work with. I plan to bring them along for the ride with me, if y'all was to ever go big with the Colombian cartel connection you make the claim of having."

Chapter 25

Good Cop-Bad Cop...

Tamron's Uncle Leroy was a leader of a tight-knit band of dirty, radical cops on the APD. It was about six of them, and what they do is, take protection pay from high profile dealers to keep them informed on everything the Atlanta Drug Task Force was up too, or had intentions to do. Say for instance, if there was to be a major raid, Leroy and company, would alert their "clients" so they could shut down their operations for a time being. Or, for extra pay, they would do small raids themselves on the competitors of the clients or even arrest the leader of a competing group. They would plant guns and drugs on them to make sure a charge was to stick. Basically a "chop off the head and the body will die" type of tactic they would use.

These dirty bastards had a method for every type of wicked scenario they were to encounter. They robbed suppliers as well and had other suppliers to sell their product for the protection and service they offered. Also, murder was a part of the business too, as Leroy and company robbed and killed in the name of power and money.

A supreme level of fear was enforced by them on the inhabitants of the ghetto. Their badges and authority transformed them into a juggernaut to be terrified of. A motherfucking beast to be reckoned with.

Leroy had power in two areas: on the force as a DT; and in the streets as a *fixer for hire*. This motherfucker was unstoppable! Not even *King Kong* had shit on him!

Tamron continued, "Well, our first batch, we got ten kilos of meth, and plenty of the other stuff, the pills and all else," Tamron revealed.

"Damn! Ten off the rip, huh! The pills and all else. Y'all got off to a good start, I see. But what y'all security look like? Because you got to have somebody toting the pistol for you out there in these vicious streets. If them wolves get a whiff of blood on y'all, or, see vulnerability outta you, they will hunt you down and won't hesitate to take you out the game! Probably faster knocking you out the game faster than you got into the game itself!" said Uncle Leroy emphatically.

"Well, my boyfriend had two of his cousins move up here to Atlanta from Albany to hold him down in those areas. And I guess I only got you. I've never gave it any thought about having a bodyguard," she said, but provided inaccurate information.

Montell had *intentions* to move his cousins to the A-town but hadn't yet.

"So, what. You don't think it's some money hungry and crazy-ass niggaz out there in the underworld, who'll kill yo ass too, for what you got—money, drugs—or for the sake of someone else?" he stated to remind her on the life she made a conscious choice to enter into.

"Oh, I totally get that part. I'm learning as I go. But it's not like anyone other than my boyfriend and you, who know of my involvement. That's exactly how I intend to keep it," she said.

"TeeTee. Let me ask you this much. Do your boyfriend know anything about me?" he demanded to know.

"Yeah, he do. He know the history of having a dad who was a cop. And he know I *had* an uncle who was one too. But no! He doesn't know *of* you by name or anything else. He thinks you retired."

"Good."

"Should I make it my business to introduce you two to one another?" she asked.

"No! Hell no! Keep it just like you got it. And remember what you just said not too long ago. *I am* your protection. And *I'm* supposed to work with you hand-in-hand. And TeeTee, rather you know it or not, you got more pull now than he do; your boyfriend. That's something you really need to keep in mind as you progress," he said to motivate his niece.

"Why you say it like that, Uncle Leroy?"

"It's because. It speaks for itself. You know the language of the connection—money and Spanish. And then, you got *me* to keep the cuffs off your wrists. But I want you to just be wise about everything and you should be all right. If you got any problems or need advice, just get in touch with me. But my shit ain't free! And this lil $25 grand you gave me off the top ain't nearly enough. I need more. And my monthly fee for you and what's your boyfriend name? Mayo?"

"It's Montell, uncle Leroy."

"Okay. *Meet-Meet* then! My fee for you and him is *six thousand* a month. That's every *first* of the month, no exceptions! Not a day late or a goddamn dollar short! You hear me what I say? And I only wanna meet up with *you* when need be. I don't *ever* wanna meet with dude. It's business now. *Big business!* And that's how it's gotta be as it relates to what we now done ventured into. It's dangerous territory for a female rookie like you in this line of work. But you know without a doubt, Uncle Leroy right here to help guide you and to protect you, just like I gave my brother and you my word I would be. Keep that in mind. Also, keep in mind, TeeTee, we only got each other. Okay, we only got each other. So, with that being said, I want you to always be mindful, you get your advice and all else that goes along with this, from me, okay. *Not* your boyfriend, and not from anyone else. *Directly* from me," he told his niece in a serious tone

"Look at me, TeeTee. This is a dirty and deadly game you done got into. You can't turn back now. Not even if you wanted so badly to. *Especially* not now, since you done been exposed to everything, and you now know everybody."

"I'm learning that now."

"But another question. At the time your boyfriend went to get the supply, were you with him?"

"I was."

"And you know the name of the connect down in Colombia and the transporter who delivered for him, do you or do you not?"

"I do." she replied again on demand.

"Okay, so see, you too far in now, TeeTee. You in the *triangle*. The triangle now, TeeTee. With the connection, the transporter. And the buyer. And with this, it's only one way in, with no way out! You're stuck. Not even if death was to claim you physically, you can't get out the life. You sold your soul to the *Devil, sweetheart*. And that greedy muthafucka, don't offer no refunds either! So be prepared to take much pride in your new life. I hope you ready, TeeTee. I hope you ready," her uncle said to her. It was more or a dire warning than anything.

The way he worded things heightened the level of suspense to it. This dramatically caused Tamron to be overcome with a minute level of fear. She dropped her head and shed a tear behind the raw reality that her uncle related.

Everything he'd said to her was the truth. The absolute truth. No jokes. She thought only in terms of living the "good life" from the fast money they were subject to make, and then, *"ride high on the hog."*

In all actuality, Tamron was completely dumbfounded about it all. This was a life she would never be able to escape. Her uncle gave her the best words of caution he was able to provide. She took heed to them, and paid attention. Hopefully she will learn a lot from him. Or else.

Leroy hugged his niece tightly and kissed her on the forehead. They were to create a bond and move forward with strength and durability in the dope game and all throughout the underworld together. They could potentially be a low-key force in the Atlanta Metropolitan area.

Chapter 26

Weeks Later...

A long awaited blessing was granted for Mandy. She managed to finally earn the promotion at the bank to the position of Bank Manager, after the retirement of Mr. Mimms. And at the same time, she'd made a mean enemy out of someone there to. They were someone who was after the same position just as much as she was. With envy and jealousy comes hatred and a storm of diabolical acts to follow to harm the other in some type of way.

Her salary greatly improved to six figures, and her line of credit through the bank, was out of this world outstanding. She was basically granted leeway to finance all she so pleased, as a house on the shore of Lake Lanier, she'd always wanted. One was now hers in ownership. She moved in promptly. In addition, she enjoyed the pleasure of paddle-boat riding almost daily. The water was only a few steps from her back door.

When she made her move, her girlfriends put together a house-warming slumber party there for them. They'd stayed up through the first night and took to the pleasures upscale life and high society had to offer. Mandy was now making it. She really was.

No doubt, Montell stayed over himself at times, as he could hardly wait to be provided a key to the house. He eventually got one. Her place was his down-low spot of residence where he was able to find solace and a peace of mind from all the madness and drama that came along with being in the dope game; part owner of a strip club with a bunch of dudes he had to constantly keep an eye on; (good friends included) and had to concern himself with ducking and dodging the law.

Montell loved to go fishing in the lake as well, as he only had to walk maybe a football field from the backdoor to the water. He'd bought a small size bass pro sporting boat. He loved to angle for this particular type of fish. Montell was from southwest Georgia and had his fair share of fishing in that part of the state. He also had to play it safe between him and Mandy on the same token. Her parents was not too fond of her being in love with a Black guy—*"a damn nigger"*—in the words of her dad.

J.D. Barfield, hated the very thought of his beloved Mandy, having the desire to be involved with a Black guy. But there was nothing he could do other than go along with it.

To avoid ever coming into contact with Montell at Mandy's house, J.D. told her he would always call long before he was to show up. He had no desire to meet her boyfriend. She agreed to the terms of her father, being she loved him and didn't ever want a confrontation to occur between the two men she loved. Mandy's mother, on the other hand had no problem with her being in an interracial relationship. She heard joy from the mouth of Mandy, also say how happy her daughter was. So, who were her parents take this happiness away? They had no right to do so. None at all.

Montell would stay over at Mandy's place for long hours throughout the day while she was at work. He had begun to stash his money there as well. It was a way safer place to keep cash there, fresh from the sell of narcotics. It would never be suspected by the cops that a black drug dealing ex-con, probation abiding, strip club owning dude, would be staying at a home in such a gated community, and putting his illicit profits away in a posh southern home owned by a *now* affluent white girl.

Montell had it made yet again, and was far more determined this time around, not to be fucked over no more like he had in the past by Verena and Eric. He mentioned her house to no one. Nobody else knew where he stayed with Mandy. And he kept his business totally to himself.

One night while staying over at Mandy's spot, they had a deep conversation over many things. This was a long-awaited conversation they both desired to have.

He initiated. "How has everything been for you at work under your new position, babe?"

"Everything been well, sweetheart. I've settled in better than I thought I would. And what about you with the business at the lounge?" she asked of him.

"The business been beautiful. We making a whole lot of money."

For quite some time since the doors opened to Seduction City, Montell has kept Mandy under the impression that all the cash he'd been turning over to her to process through the bank under the guise of investment money profited out the club, was legitimately made. This was so far from the truth.

But Montell had a clientele base of eight customers who he sold all the supply to he'd had to sell. Everything left his hands on a wholesale basis. He didn't look to make but maybe six or seven thousand dollars profit off each kilo of Meth or coke, and anywhere from five to eight dollars profit from each pill, and he had thousands of those. The Molly was a huge money-maker. There was a lot of customers that craved the addictive drug.

Montell jacked up the price on them and didn't intend to lower it under no circumstances. It was the area where Tamron played her part at, her and her girls, the *"Grade-A Clique,"* was what they called themselves. There was NeNe, Peaches, Pooh, and Kay-Kay. They sold what they had by the ounce. Tamron sold no less than a four-way though. But she kept her girls thoroughly supplied.

"I'm just glad we in a very good space in our lives and in our relationship, Montell. It's been a long time coming for us. But we here. And that's all that matters," Mandy said to Montell.

"You absolutely right about that, Mandy. You're so right about that, baby."

"So, what's the plan for us, Montell? It's time for us to excel and truly be a force in some area of life. I would think. I don't wanna continue to move without a clear outlook on where we're going. My job is gonna be there, and I'll always have employment. But I still hold aspirations to be a business owner in my own right," she related.

"I can't say right off Mandy. But truth be told, we gonna definitely be the CEO and COO of a business at some point soon. I'm eyeing maybe about a year or two from now. We can look into possibly investing in a hot start-up of some sort. But whatever our decision to put our money into, I'm sure we gonna make the best of it, no doubt," Montell said to his fair skin thick thighs having brunette.

He then kissed her, cupping her by the chin. He did so yet again, but much slower and passionately the second time. Mandy sighed sensually, as she gave in to the lustful whims she felt for Montell.

"Baby-baby-baby. Slow down a minute, okay. I have something important to share with you," she said to him.

"Oh. You do. Okay. What's up," he responded.

Mandy then got up and stepped over to the walk-in closet. When she reappeared, she had a large stuffed teddy bear wrapped in her arms. The animal had a pink and powder blue tee shirt on and a cloth pinned around the waist and lower area, as if it was a diaper. As she held on to the bear and looked at Montell in innocent fashion, she smiled graciously and awaited his response, once he was able to read between the lines.

"Sweetie, you for real?" Montell worded in an almost excited format.

Mandy smiled and then replied, "Yes baby. Yes, I am."

"So, I'm finally gonna be a daddy, huh. Finally. I feel I deserve it," he said.

"Yes, you do, baby. Yes, you do."

***

This Rat Must Die...

All the necessary paperwork had been sent where it needed to go to prove a snitch guilty. It was the witness statement forms, the signed affidavits, and all other documentations, that would show and prove indeed, Rico, aka *"Blue Dot,"* was a rat! He testified in documents. He testified on the stand against others. And he did everything else that a notorious tattletale would do to fuck over others. And now, shit was about to backfire on him.

Roderick was the one to go so far as to put to use a "Freedom of Information Act" form to get the actual trial transcript portions of Jimmy Smacks case where Rico took the stand and sung to the prosecution and the jury on him. It was like dude was Keith Sweat or Usher Raymond in their prime when he sings on those men. Roderick had Jamie, and Montell, pass off to him the documents from their discovery packages too. This helped to prove that Rico wrote statements on them too.

Through the years Rico was locked up, he tried several times to have his name legally changed but was unsuccessful at it. He did all he could to hide his true identity and conceal the vile and cutthroat things he'd done to his best friends and a man who supplied him product to make his money from to finance the businesses he had up and going.

Josh got active inside. He went to the next OG on the compound who was over the "Eight-Tre Playboy Gangsta Crips" set that Blue Dot had rank in. The OG challenged at first, because of how *solid* Blue Dot proved to be, and because of the many contributions he'd made to his gang family. But the actual court certified paperwork could not be refuted. And the OG, had no choice but to call Blue Dot—*"Rico the rat"*—out for who he truly was, a cheese eating snitch bastard! Or else, he'd be put on a plate and ate himself, for not doing so.

The Crip OG dude kept everything to himself that Josh brought to him, until the time was at hand to order something to be done. The time was ten P.M. when four veteran Crips went to confront Blue Dot and to do work. The lethal kind. He was in his cell talking on his phone when they rushed in on him.

"Nigga, get yo bitch-ass up from there!" the musclebound soldier ordered, snatching *Blue Dot* to his feet. They all had rushed in with sharp pointed shanks drawn and ready to carve dude up like a Thanksgiving Day turkey.

"Yo, what the fuck going on, cuz?" Rico asked with a look of terror in his eyes. Muscle-bound then jacked him up in the air and went to the back wall with him, hard. He then bitch-slapped Rico with a backhand and punched him in the face, knocking him to the floor, now nearly unconscious. While on the floor, muscle bound pinned Rico's head to the floor with a knee, as one of the others began to talk.

"Well-well-well, Blue Dot—*Rico*! I would have never thought of all people, *you* would be the one we found out all this snake-like shit about. You foul, nigga! Oh yeah, you really foul! But no bad deed goes unpunished, my guy. You hid it really good though," the veteran Crip said.

"Yo man, what the fuck you talking 'bout, cuz? I'm Crip for real, cuz! I'm Blue Dot! OG Blue Dot, bro! What the fuck y'all niggaz got going on?" Rico mumbled from a terrible position on the concrete floor.

"It's too late for all that shit now. You been exposed. Nigga you ate cheese on four people! We got the paperwork to prove it," said the leader of the Crips in the room.

"I don't know what you talking about, bro. Y'all got the wrong guy," he lied.

"Yeah, sure we do," the vet stated, then looked on at the other three homies he had with him, lifted his head to give them the green light to go to work. They all began to stab Rico mercilessly and with vicious force.

They were sure to poke his ass in all the areas of the body that would cause death on impact. He was hit in the neck, the left part of his torso near the heart, and in both lungs. By the time it was all said and done, they'd hit him 41 times with their sharp pointed deadly weapons. Rico was a goner. Death reached him swiftly.

They pushed his body under the bunk, then spread the blanket across so the sides of the lower bed would be covered, and the dead body not readily visible. The four then wiped their knives clean, put then bad along their waistlines, and nonchalantly walked out the room, going separate ways. It ended the run of the rat and made things much better in the world of real niggaz. Being one rat less is always better than being one rat more! Enough said.

Chapter 27

Inside Seduction City...

Geno had somehow turned really salty in a way at Jamie and crew, because they'd bullshitted him and Felix around about the paperwork of the club ownership being updated to show he were in the equation somewhere.

One night while the club was jumping and going, he pulled Jamie to the side to have a discussion about it.

"Say *shawty*, I need to chop it up with you for a moment, a'ight," Geno said to Jamie.

"Look Geno, I understand that that's how y'all talk here in Atlanta, and that's y'all lingo and all. But bruh, I'm from Duval, my nigga, and we don't agree with being called no *'shawty,'* homie. So, chill with that shit yo," said the six-foot one slim framed clean cut/clean shaven Jamie.

He looked on at Geno with those slightly bucked eyes of his and tightened his lips as he awaited some type of sarcastic response to exit Geno's mouth he knew would soon come.

"Nigga, stop being so goddamn sensitive and in ya feeling and shit behind somebody calling you by a term relevant to the times! Ol' thin-skin ass nigga! Shit ain't that serious, J. But anyway, what's the deal on the paperwork, playboy? I know it's been long enough for you to have had a lawyer look over things and next let me sign off on it so my name would be on *everything,* like you and your boy's names are," Geno said.

"I'll be sure to get around to it in due time. I've been busy with other business that need more attention at the moment. It'll be taken care of though."

"Don't worry 'bout it. I was just checking to see what lie you would throw at me next. That shit already been taken care of, nigga!"

"What?"

"Oh yeah. That's what I said. Don't you know my uncle Felix ain't no slow muthafucka.' He been felt you would try to do some underhanded shit. So he took the initiative himself and went to his people down at city hall for advice. They let him know what to do. Felix already took care of everything, my nigga. Here is a copy right here," Geno stated, then pulled a folded piece of paper from his back pocket to present to Jamie.

He accepted, unfolded and looked it over. The proper notices, certifications, and all else there was to make the document authentic.

"Yo, how the fuck is Felix gonna to take it on himself to do what *I'm* supposed to do, and don't notify me about the shit? And not only that, *he* not the one to bring it to my attention. You did! If anything, we all supposed to sit down and come to an agreement on everything," fumed Jamie.

"Nigga, you acting like we ain't already done that shit! Haven't we though? Me and unc ain't got time to play 'round with you and your little crew of niggaz, homeboy! Fuck outta here with that bullshit, my nigga! Straight up! Since unc owns thirty-five percent, the majority of the business, it gave him perfect leeway to do everything he did, since you seem to wanna bullshit my people about it," Geno said to assert the authority he now had as majority owner of Seduction City with Felix.

"I'm gonna have a talk with that nigga to see what's on his mind."

"It ain't no need to do that. What's done is done. And ain't no undoing it, you smell me, homie," Geno capped. "Now," he spoke out again, "the first order of business, on *my* watch, is this—"

"Hold up, *swoll* up! Wait a minute. What!" Jamie cut into the would be dictation of Geno.

"Need I repeat myself?" Geno commented.

"Yeah, you do. I missed the first part, my nigga."

Geno pursed his lips and cocked his head to the side as if to say, *is this nigga for real!* He then went on, "I ain't got no problem saying it again all I had just now, because I actually kinda like your style, Jamie. It's that nigga Montell, with that slick-ass mouth, I don't like! But you, you though, you cool. As I was saying, being *I'm* majority owner now, I had a few ideas to incorporate," he corrected out of respect for Jamie. A sentiment he had.

"This sounds like something that need to be brought to the attention of everybody as a whole," Jamie commented.

"Not hardly. It's a decision *I* made outside of everybody. I'm only bringing it to you because we the faces of the potential franchise, and the ones with the brains, if you stop and take timeout to see it for what it is, ole crazy-ass nigga. You can't see the forest due to the trees being in your way. Do you not realize, if you and me put our minds together, we can do some big shit? It's only incumbent we do," Geno propositioned.

Jamie furrowed his eyebrows following the words of Geno, as he seemed to be surprised at Geno's use of 'big words.' *Did this nigga just say incumbent?*

Geno, thoroughly equipped with the mental wherewithal to know how to read between the lines, had peeped game and spoke out again before Jamie could say another word

"What nigga? You think y'all the only ones smart because of the college shit you and your boys put in? Ha ha ha! You *bougie*-ass niggaz kill me with that shit. Think y'all got all the sense. But look Jamie, like I said, me and you got what it take to lead this spot to a level like no other. I just wanna know is the door open for further negotiations between you and me, and you and me only?" Geno said with his hand stretched out to be shaken by Jamie.

Jamie looked deeply into the eyes of Geno in his attempt to investigate his soul and true intent throughout his pause before agreeing to a later conversation they were intent on having. Then, reluctantly, he shook the hand of Geno, as phase one of the *mad scientist's* plan was carried out, *do whatever to get the head of the other side to sit down and talk with him and him only.* Check that box. Geno knew from that point he would be able to impose his will on Jamie without doubt.

"Now come on nigga, and let's go out here to VIP, so we can enjoy our own spot for a change. We ain't did shit but operate as niggaz over the place, and not value the pleasure we got inside it," Geno said to him causing Jamie to smile at the charisma and wit he put to good use.

They stepped side by side in suave-like fashion into the VIP section from the office and immediately began being catered to by the lovely girls who danced inside. They knew who they were. Geno had prevailed. It was an ironic turn of events with the acquaintance between the two.

Geno long ago sensed that Jamie wanted to free himself from being under the leadership that Montell made it appear he had over the entire crew and finally began to make a name and reputation for himself for a change. Geno also knew it was best to get Jamie to himself, one-on-one, and work it in that way, since Jamie was a good listener—according to Felix—and loved the art of negotiating. Now all Geno had to do was create lies and other rumors about Montell and get Jamie to believe them.

Geno noticed Jamie and Roderick appeared closer to one another than either were to Montell, as it had always been the case for years, with Montell and Eric being tighter with one another than any of the others. Rico, on the other hand was a "wild-card" so to speak and felt himself to be an outsider. That's probably why he flipped the script on them, opposite the fact of the sell to an undercover agent and him trying to get a reduced sentence. But that's neither here nor there. Geno picked up on the vulnerabilities he detected in Jamie and wanted to capitalize off them. His *mojo* was beginning to work.

Chapter 28

Montell, Tamron, and all the people they had working for them, completed the sale of all the supply they had to offer. It was time to re-up once Pete was paid the $100,000 he was owed. The money was all there, and additionally, Montell had $225,000 he wanted to spent for the second meeting, as Tamron herself, chipped in $75,000. Montell had no idea where she'd come up with it from. He became skeptical.

The lie she perpetuated to him was she had the money in a trust account in the bank left to her by her parents, which in part was true, but she hadn't touched the money, as there was no need for her to have done so. Tamron got the cash from her girlfriend who she was in a relationship with outside of what her and Montell had going on. The girlfriend, *"Lioness Karlie,"* what she called herself, an older female at forty-two, gave Tamron $30,000 of the $75K, and the other part ($15,000), came from the profit she made off retail, and from her friend, Kay-Kay ($30,000).

She (Kay-Kay) spilled the beans to her boyfriend "Black Tony," (Tony Gibson is his government) on the business her and Tamron had, and he sold all the product Kay-Kay was given to get rid of. Black, was an in the streets type nigga by far.

Tamron was close to Kay-Kay and told her about it all. Basically, ran her damn mouth a little too much. And Black Tony instructed Kay-Kay to play her role well, learn everything about the connect from Tamron as possible, and once they had stacked enough dough, then they could go to the plug themselves with the money of their own and keep shit moving like that, without Tamron or her boyfriend, Montell, knowing a fucking thing. And even if they did find out, the connect wouldn't turn them down, because of the amount of money they would be spending with them, they'd figured.

It was time to re-up, and they called Pete to set a meeting place with his people again, Javier, if possible, so hoped Tamron. She was attracted to him and the type of Latino swagger he had. During the last time they'd met up with him to get their work, Tamron, said some flirty come on things to him in Spanish. Shit she knew Montell didn't understand but she'd forgotten, Javier had Pete on video call on the lap top, and Pete heard her. He knew what she'd done and was potentially aiming to do. It wasn't good for business, and he had to see to it that this never happened again.

Once contacting Pete, he greeted Montell, "Señor Mo! *Que Pasa, Amigo!*" he said in Spanish. It's *"what's up my friend"* translated in English.

"*Que Pasa, Amigo!*" replied Montell. That was about all the Spanish he knew right there, and "*Mucho Dinero,*" which meant "lot of money."

Pete spoke to the best English of his ability. "How... ah... has... ah... life... life been treating you these... ah... days, now?"

Montell was able to comprehend his words. "Life has been good Petey. Very good," he responded.

"Great," said Pete, then immediately got down to the business at hand.

He began to speak fluently in Spanish. That was cue for Tamron to tune in and translate. Pete asked about the money owed. She let him know they had every penny of it, *plus* $225,000 more to spend. Pete smiled and congratulated them on the progress they'd begun to make.

Tamron related to Montell what was said. He smiled back at Pete and told Tamron to let him know an increase in supply on consignment would be an excellent way to congratulate him. Pete took those words as a sign of confidence and told them their wish may be granted, but he wanted to see on video call the money they had first, along with what he was owed.

"No problem, my friend," responded Tamron, then, she let Montell know what Pete asked, and they did what they were supposed to do, show the plug the money and proceed on from that point.

Pete then let them know that they would have to go to a new location, to meet up with his other people for the re-up, and it would be a new carrier this time. He was mindful how Tamron could potentially make a situation bad by her attraction to Javier, and disrespect Montell by him being ignorant of the Spanish language.

Pete needed them to meet his other people in Cobb County, Georgia, in the city of Smyrna. Just along the outskirts of there, Pete's people had a small farm. They also raised gamecocks, as the Hispanics and Latinos loved the culture and sport of it all. The directions were given to Tamron on how to get to the farm from Atlanta and when to show. The meeting was set for the upcoming Saturday at seven A.M.

***

The Re-up...

The day of the official meeting with the new distro had arrived. Montell and Tamron made it to where they needed to be. They drove in Tamron's Honda Accord, a far more discreet vehicle than Montell's Infinity.

Once inside the house, they'd met Angel and his wife, Benita. There was also an armed gunman on hand to oversee matters of security. As last time, Pete was put on video call to witness the transaction. "Greetings Señor Mo. How are you and your Señorita?" he greeted.

"We good?"

"All is well," Angel spoke pretty good English himself, so, Tamron would not be utilized as much as last time.

With his traditional Hispanic style of dress and features, Angel had on a pair of snakeskin cowboy boots with the hat and belt to match; a large oval shaped metal plate belt buckle to it, a button-down colorful shirt, a pair of blue jeans, and had a thick full mustache. Although country in fashion, Angel was clean as ever in presentation.

He took over the meeting, "Mo. Señor Pete tells me you will have roughly three hundred and twenty-five thousand dollars for me," he said to Montell.

"Yes. That's correct my friend. That's correct," Montell responded, then told them all the money was there in his bag with him.

He motioned for Tamron to pass him the mini, duffle bag. It was camouflage in color. Montell unzipped it to reveal the content. He removed the neatly wrapped bundles of cash for Angel, then sat each on the table two at a time. "It's all there, Angel. No need to count it."

Angel and his wife both smiled at Montell, then began to situate the money into a bag of their own. Angel spoke in Spanish to Pete so to let him know it was all there and he could go ahead and provide them with what they wanted. Pete agreed.

Angel then opened the bottom cabinet doors under the sink in the kitchen where they stood and removed three large sized military duffle bags. He placed them all atop the table and unzipped them one by one. Pete spoke up from the video call. The laptop was situated on the counter of the sink. He did the best he could to tell Montell in English what all he'd supplied. Then he said it in Spanish for Tamron to translate.

"Baby, Pete says there is fifty kilos of Meth, ten kilos of Molly, twenty-thousand E-Pills, twenty-thousand Percocet, and so much of the other stuff, *Flaka* and numerous packets of whole sheets of K-2 sprayed paper he meant."

Montell and Tamron both smiled. They knew it was really time to get to the money.

"Tamron, ask Pete what we owe him?"

She spoke in Spanish to Pete. He replied what his number was. "Pete says we owe him a half Million, sweetie."

Montell paused, bowed his head to think momentarily, and pinched his chin at the same time. He finally responded, "Tell him fair enough. It's a deal."

Tamron let Pete know all her man had said. Montell then saluted Pete through the screen of the laptop, and Pete disappeared.

He turned to face a smiling Angel, shook his hand as Tamron and Benita did the same, then they grabbed the bags, and made their way to the car.

Everything was put in the trunk. Montell and Tamron got in and rode off, heading back to the city to Tamron's house to begin breaking down the work and preparing it to be sold once they get there.

They'd entered into a new phase. The two transcended to a new dimension. They were all the way ready to make it do what it do. They damn sure was.

Chapter 29

The Drama Continues...

Verena and Eric seemed to be still on bad terms after the last fallout they had and his arrest in AC behind the run-in and fight with Roderick. The truth had finally been revealed to Verena about the things Eric had going on behind her back. She now knew he had another woman he was cheating on her with, and it caused her great pain emotionally. Verena had also made it her business to go online and read the newspaper for Atlantic City, so to find out exactly what happened, and who was the female her Eric was with and enjoying himself alongside in gambling haven?

She repeatedly questioned Eric but got nothing out of him. So, she took it upon herself to initiate a conversation yet again and present what she now knew about his affair and give him an ultimatum as far as their relationship was a concern.

One afternoon, it was just the two of them and their babies there at the house. Verena's mother was at the shop with her sister, and this was the time Verena needed alone with Eric, so to bring their troubles to a head and nip things in the bud. They were in the kitchen having a light meal when she got on his case.

"So, how long did you plan on not telling me anything about your little Spanish girlfriend you got?" she stated.

"What are you talking about, Verena?" he responded.

"I'm talking about the girl you was with the night you got arrested in AC, and I had to come bail your no good behind out of jail. What's here name, *Joleena*. That's what I'm talking about, Eric!" She spoke in an angry voice now.

Eric looked at her in total shook to know she was aware of Joleena's name. "I don't have a clue about a thing you talkin' 'bout."

"Oh yeah. Well, that's not what I know. And the guy you got to fighting with. He's one of your old friends, too, huh. I recognize the name from Montell's prison profile. But I'm back on the subject of Joleena. Why Eric? Why? What's so special about her to make you cheat on me with? I'm the mother of your kids?"

"I said, I don't know what you talkin' 'bout. Now let's forget 'bout it, okay."

Verena paused in speech, looked at him with her mouth wide, then squinted her eyes at him out of anger as she began to speak once more. "No! I'm not gonna forget a damn thing! It's no way I'mma sit back and allow you to dog me out like this. I'm not!" she spat, slamming a fist down hard on the table.

"Now look!" she continued. "Either you gone do right by me, or you can go ahead and pack up now and get the hell out of this house, Eric! It's on you!" A line was drawn in the sand.

"Oh, so now you ready to kick me out my own damn house, right?"

"Right!"

"All because you accusing me of something that's not true. You don't have any proof to say I've done anything. But you wanna put me out a home I helped build. Did I or did I not help put us here?" he questioned.

"That's totally beside the point, Eric. You trying to get off the subject. I said either you gonna do right by me, or you could leave. It's me or Joleena?" She reiterated herself for him.

"Hmm, you or Joleena, huh? Is that what you just said?"

"That's *exactly* what I just said. Me or your little Mexican peasant! Which one?" she said angrily and gave him a hard look. She was anticipating his reply.

Before Eric could say anything, Verena spoke out again. "What's so hard about you being a man and just saying who it is you wanna be with, Eric? Huh. Just say what need to be said and do all you feel you need to do in moving forward."

"Verena, look. I'm not trying to have this type of conversation, okay. I don't wanna talk about this," he said, trying to change the subject. But Verena was persistent and wanted to force Eric to confess in a way. She pressed him.

"Eric, rather you know it or not, I've prepared myself to move on about life without you. I'm not gonna tolerate you doing me wrong any longer. Now, I know all about your little fling you got on the side, this Joleena girl. But what I don't seem to understand is, if that's who you want, why won't you just go ahead and be with her then? Just leave me alone and go be with her."

"Where are you getting all this from anyway?"

"I read the newspaper crime section online and got everybody's name. I also found this in your pants pocket. You dirty bastard!" she stated, and tossed a small piece of paper at Eric, along with two receipts from the day he and Joleena went shopping in New York. The items purchased on the receipt was for a female, and Verena knew then, Eric had really been into dating the other one she accused him of, the Joleena girl.

"So, you go shopping at *Saks Fifth Ave* in New York and spend all this money for female designer clothing too, huh."

Eric simply sat in the highchair silently and chewed on his sandwich. He propped his arms on the countertop of the island in their kitchen.

Verena began to cry behind the thought of Eric neglecting her in exchange for another female. She got up from her seat and walked over to him. She got up in his face and began to vent yet again.

"You dirty low-down no-good bastard, you! Since you seem to be so happy with her, to take her shopping and everything else, I want you out me and my mother's house. Today! Go stay with Joleena. Better yet, why won't the two of you just go right on ahead and get a house together, because you not gonna be here no more after today."

Eric squirted his eyes and gave her a cold stare like never before. He then followed up by grabbing Verena by the sides of the head with both his hands, looked her directly in the eyes and told her straight up, "I ain't going no muthafuckin' where! What the fuck wrong with you! I'm the man! And if I wanna get a little pussy on the side, then, that's what I'll do! But you not gonna tell me, I got to leave my own house! Not the one *I* helped put you in. You got me fucked up!" he spat, then pushed her down to the tile floor as she was already melting anyway.

Verena just lay on the floor crying while Eric continued to sit and eat on the sandwich he'd made. It was a turkey and cheese with all the works.

All of a sudden, Verena sprung from the floor and began to spazz-out on him. She wailed away on with open hands. He slapped her hard with his right hand causing her to go back down to the floor holding her face in total disbelief behind the fact he'd put his hands on her.

Verena held her mouth wide and was at a loss for words to say to him. After a long moment of silence, she said something.

"Eric! You bastard! How could you! You hit me!" she shouted at him. This startled the twins in the process. They were in the bedroom sleeping but had began to cry at that point.

"You satisfied now. You made me do it. You wasn't gonna stop until you got me to react. So, there you go. I hit you," he said while still seated and drinking on the fruit punch flavored beverage he had to wash down his snack.

"Eric please, just go. Get out of my house, now!" She demanded, pointing towards the front door. "Go now, before I call the cops," she added. "Go on and be with your little Mexican girlfriend, Joleena Garcia-Diaz. You two can have each other. I should've known better anyway. Get your ass out of me and my mother's house, now, motherfucker!" she demanded, then got up from the floor and grabbed the cordless phone that was situated on the countertop.

She was about to press 9-1-1 but Eric had got up out his seat and began to gather his immediate items in preparation to leave. Verena followed him through the house the entire time, barking at him.

"You no good, low down, cheating bastard! I should've never trusted you. I should've left you alone. I knew you would turn out to be more trouble than you are worth. You better not ever come back here. And to think that I actually had good intent to be married to you some day. How stupid was I? You may as well forget about everything. Everything I said. The money, the kids, everything! You don't seem to care about the twins no way. Some father you are. You get your little rags and piece of crap phone of yours and you get out of my house!"

"I don't have no problem with that. I've got better places I could be anyway other than here where I never felt welcomed to begin with," he responded as he walked towards the front door with a lightly packed luggage in his hand.

"Well, you get on to where you feel you need to be then, mister," said Verena to the back of Eric as he left out and never looked back. She followed him all of the way to the point of him actually getting into his car, locking the door, and pulling out the driveway, en route to the other house he had. She knew nothing about this spot. It was the place where he had his supply stashed, the material he'd bought from Joleena's brother, Robert.

Eric was developing a terrible drinking problem he struggled to get a handle on. The alcohol caused him to have mood swings and a bad attitude. Verena knew that the way he consumed the dark liquor he loved, that eventually, it would become problematic and take an effect on their relationship.

She tried talking to him, also encouraged he go get treatment. But Eric only thought she was being busy trying to dictate to him and be controlling like she do, so he paid her no mind and didn't take anything she'd said of significant value.

In many ways, Eric felt relieved at the fact of he and Verena breaking up and him being out the house. He vehemently told her, *"he never felt welcomed there no way,"* and this was the opportunity he'd long awaited, so to get closer to Joleena and they begin to establish a life with each other. And not only that, Verena had nagged the hell out of him. Joleena seemed to bring him the peace he desired.

With him putting his hands on her, well, as he felt, she had it coming. She provoked him to slap her. It wasn't his intention to do so. But the fact remained, it did happen. He was definitely subject to regret ever putting his hands on an official of the state, a government agent.

Chapter 30

Later In The Day...

Eric called Joleena to come over to meet him at the place he had away from the one he lived with Verena. She was eager to see him again too, so she could ask him all about the incident in AC that led to her being arrested and facing a court date herself.

This would be her second time going to meet him there at the particular location. But his spot was good for her too, as Joleena was a private female who wanted her family knowing less of her private life as possible. She also had a few belongings at Eric's place to accommodate her stays. Mostly hygiene products and feminine care items. Joleena loved Eric's down low spot, because she could always lay back, relax, and be at ease away from the stresses of the world.

When they got done eating the Mexican styled food she brought along with her for they, they sat back on the bed to watch an episode of a TV series. It was *Slow Horses.* She wanted to talk about a few things.

"So hun, are you ready to tell me what all that was about between you and those people in Atlantic City? The fight you had with them that caused all of us to get arrested?" she asked.

"It really wasn't too much behind that, baby. Just one of my old friends I used to be cool with from years ago down in Georgia. We had a small beef behind an incident. A money dispute over a bet. He still feeling some type of way behind it, and it just so happened we bumped into one another there. As you see, he started the mess. I never meant for you to get caught up in it. I don't know why you was arrested, but they definitely should dismiss your charges."

"Oh, so that was what everything was all about, huh?"

"Yeah. That's what it was all about, Jolee."

"You mind telling me who the guy on the video call was, trash-talking you while the girl and the other guy walked behind us recording?"

Eric shrugged his shoulders and came up with something quick to tell her. Basically, the same thing, "Somebody from my past I had a beef with. All of us used to be friends at one point, but not no more. It's nothing to worry about, sweetie. Nothing to worry about. I promise you. More than likely those charges you got will be dismissed before the court date, so don't stress yourself, okay."

"I'm not. I just don't want my father or my brothers to find out anything. They'd definitely try to end what we have. No matter what business you have with them."

"Everything all good, Jolee. We good," he said as they continued to sit atop the bed and be entertained by the episode they were into.

They found comfort and relaxation anytime they were together at the house. Their plan was to eventually move in with one another. But prior to, Eric wasn't in position to do so, due to being heavily involved with Verena. This was a time past, and he made Joleena aware of the current situation he was now in.

"Joleena, from this day on, I'm probably gonna be spending more time here than at the other spot. Me and ol' girl fell out for real. We had a small fight. That was the reason I called you to come keep me company," Eric said.

"Oh really! I knew you seemed angry about something. So, she kicked you out?"

"Yep. I never felt welcomed or appreciated there no way. It was the reason I had got this spot to begin with, in the event she wanted to get stupid on me and put me out. It finally happened, and I'm here."

"Don't worry, baby. I'm here with you. I've got your back, sweetie," she assured him.

"I know you do. And that's why I'm with you," he told her and then leaned inward to give her a kiss. "Now, I've got money to make from the work I got from your bother. So let me get up and begin my day," he told her, then got to his feet and went to the bathroom to take care of his hygiene. He was followed by her.

Joleena left out the house first on her way to her and Caitlin's place, while Eric went to the closet of his room and brought out the plastic containers he had the drug supply stashed away in. He went to the dining room table with everything and began to package up different size bundles for the customers he already had lined up.

Eric loved to do business in Trenton. The majority of his clientele was there. He didn't think too much more about Verena or the fallout they had. His focus had now turned more towards Joleena and making drug deals to earn his money. He liked the power that came along in the dope game more than he did with being in the white-collar world of hustling. But no doubt about it, he would've been far better off had he made things right with Verena than allowing it to go as it had.

Chapter 31

Tamron called her uncle Leroy and welcomed him to her house. She was eager to show and prove that the movement her and her boyfriend had going on was the real deal. Not as if she needed to do so, because the uncle was already convinced she was dead-ass serious, the moment she came to him for protection, and even gave him those twenty-five G's as a deposit. This was a wise and calculated move on her part.

Montell was out and about away from her house. She had the time to have Uncle Leroy come over, show him what they were working with in the product, then have a conversation with him long before Montell was to call or decided to stop by. It was an ironic occurrence that Uncle Leroy was actually at work on the force when his niece called and requested he stop by briefly. He was to show up on lunch break.

Once he'd made it to her house, he pulled the unmarked government vehicle to the back so as to raise no suspicions. Tamron met him at the door and let him in.

"Hey, uncle Leroy," she greeted and gave him a hug.

"Hey, TeeTee. How you been?" he responded.

"I've been good. Been good. Just ready to get down to the business," she stated.

"Well, I'm here," the uncle said and was lead to one of the rooms in her house.

"We got straight again not too long ago, me and my boyfriend,"

"Oh yeah. So how has the business been going?"

"My boyfriend said, we not gonna move out and do anything just yet, until the streets dry up a bit. He says it's too plentiful right now, and he not trying to drop the price on our product."

"Sounds like to me, your little boyfriend knows what he's doing in this line of business."

Once in the bedroom, Leroy stood tall with both hands on his hips next to the large table she had in the dinning room. The area was converted to a lab for her and Montell basically.

"So, what exactly did you have you wanted to show me?"

"It's all right here," she said, then opened the door to the storage closet there, revealing the large duffle bags that was loaded with narcotics. She then began to pull them out, putting them on the table. She next unzipped them to show her uncle what the business was.

"Damn TeeTee," he exclaimed. "Y'all loaded, ain't you!" responded Leroy, as he began to put on latex gloves to examine the work.

"That's fifty kilos there. Along with ten of Molly, and an ass of different pills. I told you, we was tied in with the Colombians," she boasted.

"I see! That boyfriend of yours got it going on now, huh." He began to examine the content of the narcotics that was in the bags.

"TeeTee, now tell your uncle Leroy something, won't you. Exactly how much did y'all pay for all this shit?" He had to ask this. He looked on heavy while going through everything with a look of astonishment in his eyes.

"Actually, Uncle Leroy, we made a deposit down on it of two hundred and twenty-five thousand. But we owe the connect five hundred K in return."

"And this is your boyfriend's second time dealing with these people and they trust him like that already?"

"I told you, he and the connect brother, was real good buddies while he was in the feds. I think my boyfriend did some legal work for him and got him some type of relief in the courts, or something like that. I'm not sure. But whatever the case, that's how they developed their bond. Montell very learned in the law."

Rather she knew it or not, she'd began to empower her uncle with all the information he needed for future purpose and use. If only Tamron knew how dirty and cutthroat her uncle really was, she'd held back on some of the things she let him know and may have saved herself in a sense from being vulnerable of any potential plot or manipulation tactic that could possibly be put into play.

Although she may not have thought along those lines, just as she knew shit stinks, she couldn't fathom the thought that indeed, she could be a dispensable figure in a world that was full of wolves and sharks. Especially so with the amount of supply that her and her man was now playing with. But some people have to learn the hard way and must be taught how to value and appreciate the golden rule of silence in a game, where no man or any bitch, could be trusted.

Chapter 32

Not long before the day, there was a raid on one of the top Meth supply houses in SWATS. Four kilos of the addictive drug were seized. They had the exact type of tape and plastic packaging as the kilos uncle Leroy now had his hands on in the home of his niece. He knew the product Tamron had was pure and definitely top quality. It wasn't no way he'd reveal this to her though. Leroy's plan was to continue to play tag along, connect the dots on everything, then, in time, impose his will with the power of his authority as a detective on her. Except it will be in the underworld sense and not known around the force.

"This shit you and your boyfriend got here is the real deal, TeeTee," he said as he lifted one of the kilo packages, then placed it back down. At that moment, Tamron's cellphone ring. It was Montell calling.

"Hold tight, Uncle Leroy. This my boyfriend here calling," she worded then answered. "Hey baby! What's up," she greeted.

"Hey T-baby. What you up to?"

"Nothing too much. Not long got up and now I'm getting myself together. What's on your mind?"

"I'm down here at the club. I got one of my people here trying to do something with me. Call one of your girls for me, okay. Better yet just call NeNe. Tell her to meet you somewhere close by, not at your house, and I can have her deliver to me. My people made the wrong turn twice on the same block, but they made it all the way this time. You get me? This was a code: Someone wanted to buy two kilos of Meth and they got all the money. Give those directions to NeNe. Have her meet me at the lounge, okay. Tell her to DM me on IG when she gets close by, so I'll know, okay," he instructed.

"Montell!" Tamron shouted out of emotion.

"Look sweetie, don't start that bullshit on me, okay! I ain't got time for it, Tee. I ain't."

She kept silent and fumed inside behind the thought of Montell having the audacity to have her friend meet up with him some place without her presence, no matter what the situation was, business or otherwise.

"I'm waiting, alright. Alright," he repeated himself.

"A'ight, Montell! And this the last muthafuckin' time I'm gonna let you and that sneaky hoe NeNe, meet anywhere again, boy! You better believe that shit!" Tamron spat.

"Man, *whatever!*" Montell capped then ended the call.

She had him on speaker phone the entire time. Her uncle was able to hear the conversation between the two. He knew if TeeTee didn't get her feelings and emotions in check, she could potentially ruin everything. But that was a conversation the two of them would have another day. Not that particular one.

Tamron hated the fact Montell wanted for NeNe, to be the one to meet up with him, of all people. And knowing herself how loose and flirtatious NeNe was, especially with another woman's man, it wasn't good. This was to be the third meeting by the two, and Tamron wouldn't have it happening any longer.

"So, what was that all about?" the uncle asked.

"He got a customer who wants two kilos," she replied very casually, like it wasn't a *police officer* she was there talking to. "He wants one of my friends to deliver them. Not me," she added.

"Sounds like a smart man to me. And if you know any better, you'll find someplace else to stash all this damn narcotic. Not in your own home, TeeTee. It's not good for business. Too close for comfort. But look, the pay we spoke of, you didn't mention to your boyfriend, did you?"

"No, Uncle Leroy."

"Good. Keep it between us. Now, at some point in the future, I'm gonna need three of those to give to one of my guys I've got working for me, okay. I'll call you and let you know when and where to meet him. This is his product of choice right here," he said and pointed to the bag containing the meth. "Good ol' ice-cream. Now, I've got to go. You be easy, TeeTee. And go ahead and call your girlfriend, NeNe. Do like Montell told you," he said smiling. He hugged Tamron, kissed her on the forehead, then slowly walked to the backdoor. Tamron was calling NeNe to let her know what the business was.

Leroy wanted to be assured NeNe was on the way to meet Tamron by the time he left the house and got in his car to leave. There was a little something in mind to do.

Leroy knew his niece loved to do all of her talking on speakerphone. He wanted to hear what the two of them had to say.

NeNe answered. "Hey Tamron. What's good, girl," she greeted.

"What's good is this money I got for you to make. And what ain't good is, if my damn man keep thinking I'm gonna allow you to keep meeting up with him without me there," Tamron said.

NeNe sucked her teeth. "Girl, you bugging. I don't want no Montell, okay. It's all business, and you know that."

"Yeah, well it better be. I need you to meet me over at the McDonald's close by my house. I'll be there shortly. I got something for you to take to Montell at the club."

"And my pay?"

"Bitch you know I got that too! Don't I always?"

"Yeah, you do."

"Well, why the fuck you ask that shit then?" Tamron snapped. This was mostly from the thought of Montell having NeNe to meet him yet again.

"Tamron! Pipe down, bitch! A'ight! Pipe the fuck down, *nie!* Okay," NeNe cautioned.

"Just meet me shortly, bitch. Bye!" Tamron immediately ended the call then and there without allowing NeNe a chance to come back at her.

"You be safe, TeeTee. And be looking for my call, okay."

"Okay. I will." she responded.

He finally left out and got into his car.

Leroy next drove to an isolated spot near the highway he knew Tamron would take to get to the inner city of Atlanta from Dekalb. As he posted up and awaited, nearly thirty minutes later, Tamron passed by in her brown Jeep Cherokee, en route to go meet up with NeNe *"at the McDonalds close by her house."*

Leroy allowed Tamron the opportunity to get at a distance down the road, maybe ten car lengths, but enough to keep an eye on her direction. He pulled the unmarked car out from the space where he'd parked and followed. Tamron got to the restaurant and pulled into the lot. NeNe was already been in the area somewhere because she was there already.

Tamron parked next to NeNe's Ford Escape. Leroy was situated at the gas station convenience store. It was about two football field away, unnoticed by Tamron. He used his binoculars to watch and to also get NeNe's tag number. The color, make, and model of her vehicle was apparent.

The transaction between the two was made. Tamron got back into her Jeep and began her way in the same direction she came, as if she was going back home. Leroy allowed NeNe about ten car lengths then got behind her to follow. He made sure he had the correct tag number as he trailed, then pulled on past her and turned off, headed in the way the Department was located. His hour lunch break ended productively.

Chapter 33

Terror Strikes...

Mandy had no idea that she'd been followed for weeks by someone possibly looking to do her harm. Her stalker trailed behind for those days leading up to the present and kept close watch as she got off work at the bank and made her way home. He studied her every move and traced her very steps.

Nightfall set in on this date as the stalker intentionally transformed to a would be intruder. He parked his car along the highway that led to the community of houses lined on Lake Lanier, in Hall County Georgia residency. There was virtually zero to one percent in crime rate of the neighborhood Mandy lived. So, there was no need to have extra security on any houses owned there. Residents basically left their doors and windows unlocked, as they felt safe in their rest havens.

The intruder, dressed in all black, found an easy entry point into the home through an unlocked window in the kitchen. Mandy was upstairs in her bedroom draped in a robe and had her hair wrapped with a towel. She'd not long gotten out the shower. The house below was dimly lit. The intruder tip-toed his way across the floor, headed up the steps where the sound of the TV alerted him in the direction where someone was. As he got to the top step, he saw the bedroom door was half open with Mandy sitting atop the bed watching the TV.

Armed with a sharp eight-inch bowie knife and wickedness in his heart, he rushed through the bedroom door in his attack. Mandy was ambushed. Taken off guard. Before she had a chance to scream, he was on her.

He first punched Mandy square in the face, knocking her out with one solid blow. He had on a pair of brass knuckles. She tumbled down to the floor onto her back, and he immediately straddled atop her and socked her hard in the face once more for good measure. He then whisked out his knife, snatched her robe open to expose her breast, and cut the waist band of her panties loose, accidentally nicking the thumb of his opposite hand in the process. His blood dripped and stained the terry cloth white rope of hers and parts of her torso. He was a serial rapist wreaking havoc once more. A vicious sadistic monster on the go.

He loosened the drawstring to his sweatpants and pulled them down to his knees. Boxers included. This exposed his erect penis. The rapist-assailant lifted Mandy's legs and put them on his shoulders. He then proceeded to sexually assault her in an aggravated manner. The carnal and savage attack lasted roughly five minutes.

Once reaching his climax, he was set to ejaculate onto her mid-section. Soon thereafter, the madness prevailed. This demon began to viciously stab her in the chest. At the same time as he released, coincidentally. He yanked the remainder of her panties from around her waist to wipe his semen also the majority of his blood that leaked from his thumb.

Mandy was stabbed twelve times. She didn't stand chance of surviving. He'd murdered her outright, rather intentional or in a moment of uncontrolled chaotic panic.

With the bloody and semen soiled underwear of Mandy's still palmed in his hand he looked at her in a crazed way, from her face to her private area, then back to her face again. He pocketed the panties, stood to his feet, pulled up his own pants—blood still leaking from his thumb and dripped to the thick carpet—put his knife away, then scurried down the stairs and out the backdoor, leaving her lifeless body sprawled out on the floor in a pool of her own blood. She was thirty-five.

***

The Next Day...

Mandy didn't show up for work, as her position of Bank Manager required her to be one of the first personnel to arrive. An hour past the time she were to clock in, she still hadn't showed or called. Two hours past and no Mandy. By the time of the third hour approaching, the bank President made it his business to reach out to her. He attempted to call. He only got the voicemail. He next sent an email. Still no reply. Two more hours had passed and he repeated the process, called and emailed, emailed and called. Nothing in response by Mandy. Mr. Emerson gave it up for the day. He would simply wait for her to show the day after.

Another day approached. Still no Mandy to show at work. Mr. Emerson let only one more hour to pass before he began the repeated calls and emails. Her phone just ranged, then went to voice-mail. The emails were never replied to. Mr. Emerson began to feel like something may was wrong, since it was highly unusual for Mandy not to be present to work nor call to make her boss aware of any situation she may had faced. On Mandy's work profile, she had her parents address and phone number listed as persons to contact in case of emergency. Primarily, her father, J.D. Barfield. Mr. Emerson called him.

"J.D. Barfield here," he answered.

"Yes, Mr. Barfield. I'm Craig Emerson of First Trust Bank where your daughter Mandy works," he made him aware.

"Okay. How are you?"

"Can't complain about life. Only can deal with it. Anyway, I called because Mandy had you listed as a contact in case of emergency."

"In case of emergency!" J.D. Retorted. "So, this *must* be one?" he responded in an alarmed way and began putting on his boots and "MAGA," hat at the same time he was speaking with Mr. Emerson. JD was going over to his daughter's house to check on her personally, since he'd been alerted that the possibility of something may was wrong—an emergency of some sort.

"I can't say right off if or not this may be an emergency. But Mandy didn't show to work today, nor yesterday either."

"Oh, she didn't?" He was seriously concerned now.

"No sir. I tried to call several times but got no answer. I even sent emails. I got no replies."

"Okay, Mister Emerson, I'm gonna try to call myself. And I'm also on the way out the door now headed to her house to find out what's going on with her. I thank you for the call, okay sir."

"No problem," replied Mr. Emerson, and they concluded the call.

Soon after the call ended, J.D immediately began trying to reach Mandy by phone. Her line rang and rang and rang, then went to the voicemail. He repeated maybe ten times. All to no avail. While en route to her house, he didn't know what to think or what to believe. He sped up. Panic was setting in. He began to worry about the well-being and sake of his daughter. Nearly forty minutes later, he was pulling into the community where Mandy lived.

JD got to her house and saw her vehicle was in the driveway. He then breathes a sigh of relief at the sight of her SUV but wouldn't be really relaxed until he'd actually laid eyes on her. He parked behind the X5, got out, and walked to the front door. He pressed the doorbell once, then twice, then a third time. No answer. He then walked back to his car, wrote Mandy a quick note, returned to the front door and taped it to the handle for her to retrieve. J.D hopped into his pickup truck and then headed back home.

It was beginning to become situated in his mind maybe Mandy went into one of her mood swings yet again, to where she didn't want to be bothered with no one. Possibly her and her boyfriend had a broke up to cause her to isolate herself again. Something like she once did in high school, so thought J.D.

An hour and thirty minutes after JD left her house, in desperate need to lay eyes on her, Montell pulled up and parked behind her ride. He tried to call her twice the day before and three times this day but got no answer. He thought maybe she'd been mad at him for not calling or coming by in a couple days, due to him being caught up with Tamron and the things that they had going on.

Montell had not expected Mandy to be home at this hour in the A.M., as she would normally be at work. He had nothing to worry about though. If she was to argue once he entered the house, all he had to do was let her say all she felt like saying to get it off her mind, and all would be well from that point.

Epilogue

Never Saw This Coming...

Montell had his own key to Mandy's house. He let himself right on in with no problem. "Mandy! Mandy! You here, baby?" he called out for her. He went to the kitchen first to get a cup of juice to drink. He was thirsty. Pouring his drink, he took notice that the back door was slightly cracked open, not closed and locked as it should've been. He closed it and turned the lock to secure it.

"Mandy! You here sweetie?" Montell called out for her again. Still no answer. He grabbed a handful of grapes from the refrigerator, put them in a bowl, then headed upstairs towards the bedroom.

The TV was going and he thought Mandy may was in the room watching but ignoring him at the same time. When he got to the top step, he also noticed the bedroom door was half open as well. "Mandy, I know you hear me calling you sweetie," he said, popping grapes into his mouth one at a time and preparing his mind for a small battle of the tongues.

As he pushed the bedroom door open fully, he stopped right in his tracks in a petrified state of being. He'd never been so shook before. The bowl of grapes was freed from his hands and fell to the floor, bouncing all over the thick carpeted room. Montell stood with his mouth wide and in total shock at the terrible sight before his very eyes. He was on the brink of going into a panic, but knew he had to keep his composure in order to think his way through the situation.

196

"What the fuck!"

The gruesome sight of Mandy, his pregnant girlfriend, laid out on the floor in a pool of blood and obviously, had been sexually assaulted, immediately took a toll on Montell's mind. This set into play a path to psychological destruction at this point going forward.

"Mandy! Mandy! Mandy! Baby! What the fuck happened?" Montell said, as he leaned down and spoke to the dead body, almost touching, until he caught himself and jumped back. Mandy's cellphone rang in the moment. This instantly snapped Montell back to reality. "Oh shit! I got to hurry and get the fuck out this muthafucka!" he said to himself.

He began to pace left-to-right—out the bedroom door then back in—completely unsure on what to do next. Her phone momentarily stopped ringing, then began to ring once more. It had also beep and buzz from the many notifications that passed through.

Montell wished like all hell he hadn't been the one to have found her in the way she was. But it was too late for that. "FUCK!" he shouted, then put both his hands atop his head while still pacing and desperately trying to figure out a way to get the hell on without it ever being known he had been there.

"Fuck that! I'm out this muthafucka!" he said to himself again, then ran out the room, down the stairs, and out the door to get in his car and get the fuck away from the crime scene as fast as he could.

If anyone had taken notice Montell and the way he bailed the hell out the house, they'd swear before God, that *he* was the one that had committed the crime. But it was a far cry from the actual truth.

Rather Montell actually knew it or not, he did have a witness who saw him vividly enter her home and exit in the fast manner he had. Mandy had the "Ring" doorbell security system installed on her home. Mail pirating was on the rise and Mandy almost always ordered items and merchandise from Amazon.

The surveillance system captured everything. The only problem with that was, the installation was only about eighty-five percent complete and had no camera on the backside of the home. Had this been so, it would have captured the intruder/killer, creeping in and running out. But it didn't. And now, Montell was in a world of trouble. He inadvertently placed himself in this situation.

As he drove towards his place, panic began to seriously set in. The man had no clue on what to do next. So, he followed his instincts and did what any logical minded person would do, especially a man in this instance. He called his mother.

"Hello," the mother answered.

"MA! Ma! I got a serious problem! A really serious one. I'll be down there today, okay. In the next few hours," Montell said to her.

"Baby, what's wrong. Talk to me!" she responded.

"I can't talk over the phone, ma. I'll tell you everything when I get there. I got to go, okay. I got to go ma," he said and ended the call with her, leaving the lady worried sick about her only son.

I don't know what the fuck to do. Should I call 9-1-1? Should I not? Or what should I do? Montell thought hard and deep to himself. *I wonder who the fuck did that to my sweetie? Who would wanna kill Mandy? And she pregnant too! This shit too much for me right about now. Too fucking much!* he further thought.

As bad as he wanted to, Montell held back the tears in crying. He truly wanted to do something to help his dear Mandy at the point of seeing her laid out on the floor in the way she was. But Montell also knew the best thing to do was not to touch anything as he'd steered away from doing.

DAMN! I shouldn't have left her like that. I shouldn't have. The least I could've done is call someone to go to the house to get her. What if she was still alive? Maybe she wasn't dead. I got something now in mind I can do.

He pulled out one of his six cellphones, powered it, and dialed 9-1-1. The operator answered,

"Hello. Nine-one-one! What's your emergency?" she asked.

In the best and deepest disguised voice he could, he reported to the operator. "Yes ma'am. I don't know how to say this, but I'm the cable guy at a home. And as I was working, I heard a gunshot inside of the homes," he'd said.

"Okay, and where is this location?"

Montell provided Mandy's home address as he knew it by heart.

"It could be a case of suicide ma'am. I can't say right off. Bye," he lastly stated and pressed **END** on the phone, took out the battery and SIM card, and continued to drive towards his house. He put the phone in a bag he'd had food in, and as he got close to his spot, he stopped at a dumpster near an apartment complex. Montell tossed the bag inside and kept going to his house.

As he made it inside, he was now hellbent to grab a few things to hold him over a couple days, something hit him. *Dammit! How the fuck did I forget about that?* He'd gotten pissed and scolded himself.

Montell was subject to be in an additional world of trouble atop of possibly being the main suspect in a rape-homicide once the police get to the house. The problem was, he'd not long before the day, stashed five kilos of Meth, two of Molly, a few guns, and $80,000 at Mandy's house in the laundry room. It was too late to try to go and get it out the house at that point.

The police was definitely on the way behind 9-1-1 call he made. His reality quickly become one he began to dread and hate. Even if he was not accused of or arrested on the murder or *attempted murder* of Mandy (he didn't know if she was dead or still alive), he would still end up going to jail on drug related charges, he thought. Once a search was to take place—a certain course of action—the police would definitely locate everything in the home. But in Georgia, possession of anything is nine tenths of the law. And a person must be caught with something damn near red handed, for a possession charge to stick.

But how could he get around the fact he was the boyfriend of Mandy and the only possible one to have placed all the illegal contraband in her home? Now that, was the "Billion Dollar Riddle" Montell would have to figure out.

Once he got to his house, he went to the mini safe he had, got all of his money and jewelry out of it, grabbed a few pieces of clothes and other things, then rushed back out the door, got in his vehicle, and headed towards Tamron's house.

To Be Continued...

ABOUT THE AUTHOR

PRINCE, is a writer of gritty, raw, dark, and suspenseful contemporary urban/street crime fiction. The works of his, embody American society and African-American culture, as is, in the way that it is. Nothing less. Nothing more. The characters he creates, are realistic in nature, in all of their wiles and ways. The style of writing Prince has developed, speaks for itself. You're drawn in the more and more you read, until you're locked there; with one way in and no way out. In a word to describe his skills within the craft: it's **LETHAL.**

Prince, vehemently declares at every opportunity that, *"WRITING, IS HIS ONLY SALVATION!"* He stands firmly on business with this.

The works he's released thus far in addition to this, is the popular **BLOODLINE OF A SAVAGE** series (three installments to date); **THESE VICIOUS STREETS** series (three installments to date); and the **RELENTLESS GOON** series; (three installments to date) to name a few. More captivating stories are on the way.

Prince is currently hard at work on his next installment to the story you've just read. Look forward to new releases from him soon. He highly encourages feedback and engaging conversation about his books in general and the writing industry as a whole. You may contact him at the following:

PRINCE A. TAUHID #952058
MACON STATE PRISON
P.O. BOX 426
OGLETHORPE, GEORGIA 31068
iamprinceforever3000@gmail.com

The Pen Is Mightier Than The Pistol
EMBRACE WRITING!

Lock Down Publications and Ca$h Presents
Assisted Publishing Packages

Due to an increase in the price of services we have increased our prices. The prices below reflect the price increase as of 11/1/24.

BASIC PACKAGE	UPGRADED PACKAGE
$699	**$1000**
Editing	Typing
Cover Design	Editing
Formatting	Cover Design
	Formatting
	Upload eBooks to Amazon
	Upload Paperback to Amazon
ADVANCE PACKAGE	**LDP SUPREME PACKAGE**
$1,400	**$1,700**
Typing	Typing
Editing (line editing/content)	Editing (line editing/content)
Cover Design	Cover Design
Formatting	Formatting
Copyright Registration	Copyright Registration
Proofreading	Proofreading
Upload eBooks to Amazon	Set up Amazon Account
Upload Paperback to Amazon	Upload eBooks to Amazon
	Upload Paperback to Amazon
	Advertise on LDP's Amazon and Facebook Page

***

Other services available upon request.
Additional charges may apply

Lock Down Publications
P.O. Box 944
Stockbridge, GA 30281-9998
Phone: 470 303-9761
Email: lockdownpublications@gmail.com

Submission Guideline

Submit the first three chapters of your completed manuscript to ldpsubmissions@gmail.com. In the subject line add **Your Book's Title**. The manuscript must be in a Word Doc file and sent as an attachment. Document should be in Times New Roman, double spaced, and in size 12 font. Also, provide your synopsis and full contact information. If sending multiple submissions, they must each be in a separate email.

Have a story but no way to send it electronically? You can still submit to LDP/Ca$h Presents. Send in the first three chapters, written or typed, of your completed manuscript to:

LDP: Submissions Dept
P.O. Box 944
Stockbridge, GA 30281-9998

DO NOT send original manuscript. Must be a duplicate. Provide your synopsis and a cover letter containing your full contact information.

Thanks for considering LDP and Ca$h Presents.

NEW RELEASES

BLOODLINE OF A SAVAGE 1-3
THESE VICIOUS STREETS 1-3
RELENTLESS GOON 1-3
BY PRINCE A. TAUHID

THE BUTTERFLY MAFIA 1-3
BY FUMIYA PAYNE

A THUG'S STREET PRINCESS 1&2
BY MEESHA

CITY OF SMOKE 3
BY MOLOTTI

GET IT IN SLUGS 1 &2
BY B. STALL

STANDING ON HER BUSINESS 1&2
BY DG SANTANA

STEPPERS 1,2&3
THE REAL BADDIES OF CHI-RAQ
BY KING RIO

THE LANE 1&2
BY KEN-KEN SPENCE

THUG OF SPADES 1&2
LOVE IN THE TRENCHES 2
CORNER BOYS
BY COREY ROBINSON

TIL DEATH 3
BY ARYANNA

THE BIRTH OF A GANGSTER 4
BY DELMONT PLAYER

PRODUCT OF THE STREETS 1-3
BY DEMOND "MONEY" ANDERSON

NO TIME FOR ERROR
BY KEESE

MONEY HUNGRY DEMONS 1-2
BY TRANAY ADAMS

HUB CITY MENACE 1-3
BY J. WHITE

A THUGGISH PASSION 1&2
LAND OF DA HOOLIGANZ 1-4
KILLAZ ON STANDBY 1&2
BY IRA B.

FO'EVA ROLLIN 1&2
BY ASSA RAYMOND BAKER

THE LEVEL UP 1&3
BY LUXURY KING

Coming Soon from Lock Down Publications/Ca$h Presents

IF YOU CROSS ME ONCE 6
ANGEL V
By Anthony Fields

A THUGS STREET PRINCESS 3
By Meesha

CORNER BOYS 2
By Corey Robinson

THA TAKEOVER
By Keith Chandler

BETRAYAL OF A G 2
By Ray Vinci

SAVAGE FAMILY EMPIRE 1&2
SOULLESS GOON 1,2&3
THE DIRTY SIDE OF MONEY 1,2&3
By Prince

FOR MY ENEMY'S SAKE
AMBITIONS OF A SLIDER
FRESH OFF DA PORCH
By IRA B.

THE TRUCKLOAD 1-4
TIPPIN' THE SCALES 1-3
BAD BITCHES WIT GUNZ 3
PROBLEM SOLVED 2
By Christopher "Diesel" Hornezes

Available Now

RESTRAINING ORDER 1 & 2
By **CA$H & Coffee**

LOVE KNOWS NO BOUNDARIES 1-3
By **Coffee**

RAISED AS A GOON I, II, III & IV
BRED BY THE SLUMS I, II, III
BLAST FOR ME I & II
ROTTEN TO THE CORE I II III
A BRONX TALE I, II, III
DUFFLE BAG CARTEL I II III IV V VI
HEARTLESS GOON I II III IV V
A SAVAGE DOPEBOY I II
DRUG LORDS I II III
CUTTHROAT MAFIA I II
KING OF THE TRENCHES
By **Ghost**

LAY IT DOWN I & II
LAST OF A DYING BREED I II
BLOOD STAINS OF A SHOTTA I & II III
By **Jamaica**

LOYAL TO THE GAME I II III
LIFE OF SIN I, II III
By **TJ & Jelissa**

IF LOVING HIM IS WRONG…I & II
LOVE ME EVEN WHEN IT HURTS I II III
By **Jelissa**

PUSH IT TO THE LIMIT
By **Bre' Hayes**

BLOODY COMMAS I & II
SKI MASK CARTEL I, II & III
KING OF NEW YORK I II, III IV V
RISE TO POWER I II III
COKE KINGS I II III IV V
BORN HEARTLESS I II III IV
KING OF THE TRAP I II
By **T.J. Edwards**

WHEN THE STREETS CLAP BACK I & II III
THE HEART OF A SAVAGE I II III IV
MONEY MAFIA I II
LOYAL TO THE SOIL I II III
By **Jibril Williams**

A DISTINGUISHED THUG STOLE MY HEART I II & III
LOVE SHOULDN'T HURT I II III IV
RENEGADE BOYS 1-4
PAID IN KARMA 1-3
SAVAGE STORMS 1-3
AN UNFORESEEN LOVE 1-3
BABY, I'M WINTERTIME COLD 1-3
A THUG'S STREET PRINCESS 1&2
By **Meesha**

A GANGSTER'S CODE 1-3
A GANGSTER'S SYN 1-3
THE SAVAGE LIFE 1-3
CHAINED TO THE STREETS 1-3
BLOOD ON THE MONEY 1-3
A GANGSTA'S PAIN 1-3
BEAUTIFUL LIES AND UGLY TRUTHS
CHURCH IN THESE STREETS
By **J-Blunt**

CUM FOR ME 1-8
An LDP Erotica Collaboration

THE DIRTY SIDE OF MONEY 2 | PRINCE

BLOOD OF A BOSS 1-5
SHADOWS OF THE GAME
TRAP BASTARD
By **Askari**

THE STREETS BLEED MURDER 1-3
THE HEART OF A GANGSTA 1-3
By **Jerry Jackson**

WHEN A GOOD GIRL GOES BAD
By **Adrienne**

THE COST OF LOYALTY 1-3
By **Kweli**

BRIDE OF A HUSTLA 1-3
THE FETTI GIRLS 1-3
CORRUPTED BY A GANGSTA 1-4
BLINDED BY HIS LOVE
THE PRICE YOU PAY FOR LOVE 1-3
DOPE GIRL MAGIC 1-3
By **Destiny Skai**

A KINGPIN'S AMBITION
A KINGPIN'S AMBITION II
I MURDER FOR THE DOUGH
By **Ambitious**

TRUE SAVAGE 1-7
DOPE BOY MAGIC 1-3
MIDNIGHT CARTEL 1-3
CITY OF KINGZ 1&2
NIGHTMARE ON SILENT AVE
THE PLUG OF LIL MEXICO 1&2
CLASSIC CITY
By **Chris Green**

A GANGSTER'S REVENGE 1-4
THE BOSS MAN'S DAUGHTERS 1-5
A SAVAGE LOVE 1&2
BAE BELONGS TO ME 1&2
A HUSTLER'S DECEIT 1-3
WHAT BAD BITCHES DO 1-3
SOUL OF A MONSTER 1-3
KILL ZONE
A DOPE BOY'S QUEEN 1-3
TIL DEATH 1-3
IMMA DIE BOUT MINE 1-6
DYING FOR LIKES
By **Aryanna**

A DOPEBOY'S PRAYER
By **Eddie "Wolf" Lee**

THE KING CARTEL 1-3
By **Frank Gresham**

THESE NIGGAS AIN'T LOYAL 1-3
By **Nikki Tee**

GANGSTA SHYT 1-3
By **CATO**

THE ULTIMATE BETRAYAL
By **Phoenix**

BOSS'N UP 1-3
By **Royal Nicole**

I LOVE YOU TO DEATH
By **Destiny J**

I RIDE FOR MY HITTA
I STILL RIDE FOR MY HITTA
By **Misty Holt**

LOVE & CHASIN' PAPER
By **Qay Crockett**

TO DIE IN VAIN
SINS OF A HUSTLA
By **ASAD**

BROOKLYN HUSTLAZ
By **Boogsy Morina**

BROOKLYN ON LOCK 1 & 2
By **Sonovia**

GANGSTA CITY
By **Teddy Duke**

A DRUG KING AND HIS DIAMOND 1-3
A DOPEMAN'S RICHES
HER MAN, MINE'S TOO 1&2
CASH MONEY HO'S
THE WIFEY I USED TO BE 1&2
PRETTY GIRLS DO NASTY THINGS
By **Nicole Goosby**

LIPSTICK KILLAH 1-3
CRIME OF PASSION 1-3
FRIEND OR FOE 1-3
By **Mimi**

TRAPHOUSE KING 1-3
KINGPIN KILLAZ 1-3
STREET KINGS 1&2
PAID IN BLOOD 1&2
CARTEL KILLAZ 1-3
DOPE GODS 1&2
By **Hood Rich**

THE STREETS ARE CALLING
By **Duquie Wilson**

STEADY MOBBN' 1-3
THE STREETS STAINED MY SOUL 1-3
By **Marcellus Allen**

WHO SHOT YA 1-3
SON OF A DOPE FIEND 1-4
HEAVEN GOT A GHETTO 1&2
SKI MASK MONEY 1&2
By **Renta**

GORILLAZ IN THE BAY 1-4
TEARS OF A GANGSTA 1/&2
3X KRAZY 1&2
STRAIGHT BEAST MODE 1&2
By **DE'KARI**

TRIGGADALE 1-3
MURDA WAS THE CASE 1-3
By **Elijah R. Freeman**

SLAUGHTER GANG 1-3
RUTHLESS HEART 1-3
By **Willie Slaughter**

GOD BLESS THE TRAPPERS 1-3
THESE SCANDALOUS STREETS 1-3
FEAR MY GANGSTA 1-5
THESE STREETS DON'T LOVE NOBODY 1-2
BURY ME A G 1-5
A GANGSTA'S EMPIRE 1-4
THE DOPEMAN'S BODYGAURD 1&2
THE REALEST KILLAZ 1-3
THE LAST OF THE OGS 1-3
By **Tranay Adams**

MARRIED TO A BOSS 1-3
By **Destiny Skai & Chris Green**

KINGZ OF THE GAME 1-7
CRIME BOSS 1-4
By **Playa Ray**

FUK SHYT
By **Blakk Diamond**

DON'T F#CK WITH MY HEART 1&2
By **Linnea**

ADDICTED TO THE DRAMA 1-3
IN THE ARM OF HIS BOSS
By **Jamila**

LOYALTY AIN'T PROMISED 1&2
By **Keith Williams**

YAYO 1-4
A SHOOTER'S AMBITION 1&2
BRED IN THE GAME
By **S. Allen**

TRAP GOD 1-3
RICH $AVAGE 1-3
MONEY IN THE GRAVE 1-3
CARTEL MONEY 1&2
By **Martell Troublesome Bolden**

FOREVER GANGSTA 1&2
GLOCKS ON SATIN SHEETS 1&2
By **Adrian Dulan**

TOE TAGZ 1-4
LEVELS TO THIS SHYT 1&2
IT'S JUST ME AND YOU
By **Ah'Million**

KINGPIN DREAMS 1-3
RAN OFF ON DA PLUG
By **Paper Boi Rari**

THE STREETS MADE ME 1-3
By **Larry D. Wright**

CONFESSIONS OF A GANGSTA 1-4
CONFESSIONS OF A JACKBOY 1-3
CONFESSIONS OF A HITMAN
CONFESSIONS OF A DOPE BOY
By **Nicholas Lock**

I'M NOTHING WITHOUT HIS LOVE
SINS OF A THUG
TO THE THUG I LOVED BEFORE
A GANGSTA SAVED XMAS
IN A HUSTLER I TRUST
By **Monet Dragun**

QUIET MONEY 1-3
THUG LIFE 1-3
EXTENDED CLIP 1&2
A GANGSTA'S PARADISE
By **Trai'Quan**

CAUGHT UP IN THE LIFE 1-3
THE STREETS NEVER LET GO 1-3
By **Robert Baptiste**

NEW TO THE GAME 1-3
MONEY, MURDER & MEMORIES 1-3
By **Malik D. Rice**

CREAM 2-3
THE STREETS WILL TALK
By **Yolanda Moore**

THE STREETS WILL NEVER CLOSE 1-3
By **K'ajji**

LIFE OF A SAVAGE 1-4
A GANGSTA'S QUR'AN 1-4
MURDA SEASON 1-3
GANGLAND CARTEL 1-3
CHI'RAQ GANGSTAS 1-4
KILLERS ON ELM STREET 1-3
JACK BOYZ N DA BRONX 1-3
A DOPEBOY'S DREAM 1-3
JACK BOYS VS DOPE BOYS 1-3
COKE GIRLZ
COKE BOYS
SOSA GANG 1&2
BRONX SAVAGES
BODYMORE KINGPINS
BLOOD OF A GOON
By **Romell Tukes**

CONCRETE KILLA 1-3
VICIOUS LOYALTY 1-3
BLOODY MONEY BAGS
By **Kingpen**

THE ULTIMATE SACRIFICE 1-6
KHADIFI
IF YOU CROSS ME ONCE 1-3
ANGEL 1-4
IN THE BLINK OF AN EYE
By **Anthony Fields**

THE LIFE OF A HOOD STAR
By **Ca$h & Rashia Wilson**

NIGHTMARES OF A HUSTLA 1-3
BLOOD AND GAMES 1&2
By **King Dream**

GHOST MOB
By **Stilloan Robinson**

HARD AND RUTHLESS 1&2
MOB TOWN 251
THE BILLIONAIRE BENTLEYS 1-3
REAL G'S MOVE IN SILENCE
By **Von Diesel**

MOB TIES 1-7
SOUL OF A HUSTLER, HEART OF A KILLER 1-3
GORILLAZ IN THE TRENCHES
OOPS CRY TOO 1&2
THE DAUGHTER OF A CARTEL BOSS
By **SayNoMore**

BODYMORE MURDERLAND 1-3
THE BIRTH OF A GANGSTER 1-4
By **Delmont Player**

FOR THE LOVE OF A BOSS 1&2
By **C. D. Blue**

KILLA KOUNTY 1-5
TENDER
By **Khufu**

MOBBED UP 1-4
THE BRICK MAN 1-5
THE COCAINE PRINCESS 1-10
STEPPERS 1-3
SUPER GREMLIN 1-4
A GANGSTA'S SON
By **King Rio**

MONEY GAME 1&2
By **Smoove Dolla**

A GANGSTA'S KARMA 1-5
By **FLAME**

KING OF THE TRENCHES 1-3
By **GHOST & TRANAY ADAMS**

BAD BITCHES WIT GUNZ 1&2
PROBLEM SOLVED
By "Christopher Diesel" Hornezes

QUEEN OF THE ZOO 1&2
By **Black Migo**

GRIMEY WAYS 1-3
BETRAYAL OF A G
By **Ray Vinci**

XMAS WITH AN ATL SHOOTER
By **Ca$h & Destiny Skai**

KING KILLA 1&2
By **Vincent "Vitto" Holloway**

BETRAYAL OF A THUG 1&2
By **Fre$h**

COUNTDOWN OF A KILLA 1&2
SEX, MURDER AND GOD 1&2
GUNS DOWN, BOTTOMS UP 1&2
By Lo-Life

THE MURDER QUEENS 1-7
By **Michael Gallon**

FOR THE LOVE OF BLOOD 1-4
By **Jamel Mitchell**

THE DIRTY SIDE OF MONEY 2 | PRINCE

HOOD CONSIGLIERE 1&2
NO TIME FOR ERROR
By **Keese**

PROTÉGÉ OF A LEGEND 1,2&3
LOVE IN THE TRENCHES 1&2
By **Corey Robinson**

THE PLUG'S RUTHLESS DAUGHTER 1&2
By **Tony Daniels**

BORN IN THE GRAVE 1-3
CRIME PAYS
By **Self Made Tay**

MOAN IN MY MOUTH
By **XTASY**

TORN BETWEEN A GANGSTER AND A GENTLEMAN
By **J-BLUNT & Miss Kim**

LOYALTY IS EVERYTHING 1-3
CITY OF SMOKE 1-3
By **Molotti**

HERE TODAY GONE TOMORROW 1&2
By **Fly Rock**

WOMEN LIE MEN LIE 1-4
FIFTY SHADES OF SNOW 1-3
STACK BEFORE YOU SPLURGE
GIRLS FALL LIKE DOMINOES
NAÏVE TO THE STREETS
By **ROY MILLIGAN**

PILLOW PRINCESS
By **S. Hawkins**

THE DIRTY SIDE OF MONEY 2 | PRINCE

THE BUTTERFLY MAFIA 1-3
SALUTE MY SAVAGERY 1&2
By **Fumiya Payne**

THE LANE 1&2
By Ken-Ken Spence

THE PUSSY TRAP 1-5
By **Nene Capri**

DIRTY DNA
By **Blaque**

SANCTIFIED AND HORNY
by **XTASY**

BOOKS BY LDP'S CEO, CA$H

TRUST IN NO MAN
TRUST IN NO MAN 2
TRUST IN NO MAN 3
BONDED BY BLOOD
SHORTY GOT A THUG
THUGS CRY
THUGS CRY 2
THUGS CRY 3
TRUST NO BITCH
TRUST NO BITCH 2
TRUST NO BITCH 3
TIL MY CASKET DROPS
RESTRAINING ORDER
RESTRAINING ORDER 2
IN LOVE WITH A CONVICT
LIFE OF A HOOD STAR
XMAS WITH AN ATL SHOOTER